A spaceship is sent to a moon called Heja to find plants that can be used to cure cancer. The spaceship crash-lands on this celestial body. The crew must find a way to escape because dangerous beasts roam its jungles and deserts.

A Moon Called Heja
Copyright © 2020 Thadd Evans
ISBN: 978-1-4874-3055-9
Cover art by Martine Jardin

Published by eXtasy Books Inc or
Devine Destinies, an imprint of eXtasy Books Inc

Look for us online at:
www.eXtasybooks.com or www.devinedestinies.com

A Moon Called Heja

By

Thadd Evans

DEDICATION

Jules Vern

CHAPTER ONE

It was the year 5014 on my home planet, Afan. I entered my supervisor's office.

His name was Delm and he was frowning.

"Tom, I have a new assignment for you."

"Okay." I sat down, my mind racing, wondering what he would say.

"Nen Pharmaceuticals and GSA want to send a spacecraft to Heja because fourteen plants on it can be used to cure eight types of cancer."

I shivered, a nervous response. GSA, short for the Global Space Agency, built most of this planet's interstellar craft. Three months ago, satellites had discovered Heja, a moon that was five light years away from us.

"You're a great pilot."

"Thanks."

"The first interview will be with a copilot, a shape-shifting robot called Eve. She is a new prototype called TAS, short for Technical Assistant."

My stomach tightened. Too many androids broke down in jungles, oceans, and other places. "Is she durable?"

"You're experienced. Figure that out for yourself."

I recoiled, showing irritation. He didn't answer my question. If she broke down, would they tell me it was my fault because I picked a flawed android?

He clenched his teeth and said, "Then go to different jungles and deserts to interview the rest of the crew. Observe them, talk to them. Are they suitable? If not, find the best."

"Okay."

"Nen and GSA have spent a lot of money on this."

"When do I leave?"

"In a few minutes. I just sent more information into your contact lenses and your nanites."

Years ago, GSA and MAA—Mind Adapt Agency, had injected nanites into my bloodstream. These tiny robots improved my ability to solve complicated questions. "Will the war in Keer spread?" Keer, a country, was on the opposite side of Afan.

He frowned. "I doubt it."

I stood and exited the room, information appearing in my lenses.

Xann Manufacturing created Eve. This company had produced fifteen different prototypes in the last sixty years.

I left the building, stepped inside a celestial craft, waved my hand over a control panel and the ship took off.

Eventually, I entered Xann. A tall Qio humanoid male with orange skin, a stranger in a suit said, "Welcome. Come with me."

"When will I meet Eve?"

He grinned. "In a short while."

Both of us walked past android heads, feet, hands, ears, eyeballs, and fingers, all of them on shelves. He pointed at them. "These are some examples of what we produce. Each body part is custom made."

I sighed, bored. "Thanks." Up ahead, a white woman in a gray uniform jumped upward sixty feet and landed on a balcony.

The man pointed at her. "She is adaptable."

I nodded.

Without warning, the man changed into a beautiful, five-foot eight-inch tall white woman. "I am Eve."

I blinked, surprised.

She asked in a flat tone, "Why are you here?"

I answered, "I am traveling to a moon called Heja to find plants that can be used to cure cancer, and I need a crew."

"My supervisor told me about your journey. I would be an outstanding crewmember. It is time to depart."

"What kind of aircraft can you fly?"

"SC, IC, FC, and six other types."

"Great." Stellar Craft was designed to fly around planets and moons. Interstellar Craft traveled between these. Flexible Craft went around moons, planets, and between them. "How many times have you flown in three-D holographic environments?"

"Two hundred."

"Outstanding. How many times have you flown around real planets, moons, and between them?"

"Never."

I paused, my jaw muscles tight.

"Judging by that expression on your face, my lack of experience in the real world bothers you."

"It does."

"Sorry to disappoint."

I exhaled, trying to relax.

"Are you going to hire me?"

"Maybe."

She looked straight ahead, a blank expression on her face.

"Do you have an FC on you?"

"Affirmative."

"Let's go outside and leave."

The craft shot out of her neck and we stepped inside the flying machine.

She said, "This ship is called Bright Spirit."

"Do your contact lenses have panels that control it?"

"My optic nerves control it."

"Amazing. I've never heard of an optic nerve doing that."

"This tool is three weeks old."

"Has it been tested in the real world?"

"Only in three-D holographic environments."

I cringed. "How many times has it been tested in those environments?"

"Nineteen."

My breathing sped up, a worried response. "The tool should have been tested at least thirty times."

"Of course."

I paused, trying to relax.

"Judging by that expression on your face, you don't think I can fly this."

"You could say that."

"Do you want me to fly it?"

Chills ran up my spine. "Go ahead."

Bright Spirit rose and sped up. "Impressive."

Eve blinked.

"Do you like compliments?" Because she remained stony-faced it was hard to tell if this achievement pleased her.

"I'm trying to get used to them. By the way, I just exported data into your optic nerve. From this point on a control panel will appear in your field of vision. You can use that panel to fly Bright Spirit."

"Thanks. You're hired."

She offered a slight nod, one that was barely noticeable.

"The next step is interviewing Dr. Gary Lake. He is a geneticist and an animal behavior scientist who studies lemurs in the Disig."

"The Disig Jungle is three thousand two hundred miles north of here."

"Correct. Is that information in your lenses?"

"It is."

"You imported that data in less than a second, faster than anybody I've ever met."

She kept staring straight ahead. In her pupils, white lines raced from top to bottom, indicating that she was organizing graphs. "I'm well designed. Archives indicate that you have flown between Iap, Ejj, Yela, and Afan eighty-one times."

"Yes."

"You have twelve years' experience piloting SC, IC, FC, space schooners, Afan Air Force interstellar personnel carriers, and Debban Corporation Planetary vessels. You received a bachelor's degree in Aeronautics from Maen Academy, a college in United Provinces. United Provinces is on the Rooss, a continent in Afan's western hemisphere.

After that, you attended Coro, a university in the Republic of Goln, a country in Afan's southern hemisphere. Within two years, you received a master's degree in Flight Path Algorithms, graduating fourth in a class of ninety."

I blinked, amazed. "You are well informed."

"My bio-logic boards are linked to six internal quantum computers."

"A team of software engineers and bio-physicists worked hard to create you."

"An accurate statement."

Gary's resume appeared in my lenses. This scientist, who was born in the United Territories, a country on Kak, and an island Afan's northern hemisphere, was the oldest of three children. His father was a high school a math instructor. His mother worked part-time in a middle school, teaching physics.

At the age of six, he began studying wasps. For the next several years collected them, wanting to how they communicated with each other and what techniques they used to locate food.

He attended Snet, a college in the Republic of Cern, a

country that was close to the United Territories. After three years of endless cramming, he received his bachelor's degree in Insect Genome Arrangement, graduating fourth in a class of two thousand.

After receiving his diploma, he entered graduate school at Raeg, a university in the United Territories. After one year he received a master's degree in Insect Base Pair Manipulation, graduating with honors. After applying to several schools, he was accepted by Tolo, a university in the United Territories.

Three years later, he received a doctorate in Entomology, graduating Cum Laude. Several of his classmates described him as articulate, driven. A few weeks after receiving his diploma, Izat, a corporation in the United Provinces hired him. The text vanished because no more information was available.

I said, "Eve, Gary hasn't responded to my emails, three-D holographic, or text messages."

"He hasn't answered mine either."

"Are his contact lenses working normally?"

"A perceptive question."

Within the hour, I broke into a cold sweat. "The map shows that we're headed for a hurricane."

"A valid statement."

"The database offers dangerous routes. Is there a better way to get around the storm?"

"If we fly over it, there is a thirty-two percent chance of reaching our destination."

My adrenaline pumped faster. "Can you handle it?"

"By all means."

Bright Spirit zoomed upward. High winds knocked us to the right. I grimaced. "According to three-D holographic maps, The Disig is huge, over four million square miles."

"There are ten thousand, four hundred insect species in it.

However, two hundred entomologists have admitted there are at least eight thousand more. Because too many entomologists ended up with yellow fever or other diseases, many realize that going there is dangerous."

I cringed

CHAPTER TWO

Bright Spirit raced downward, went between towering kapoks, halted, then dropped. Cables shot out of its belly and
attached themselves to nearby lupuna, gigantic trees that
blocked out most of the sky. I asked, "Can't you land closer to
the ground?"

"That is impossible. This is the best spot. Gary and his team
are two miles away, camped out in one of the denser parts of
the jungle. If we touched down in other locations, he would
be either five or eight miles away."

I paused, my jaw muscles tensed, disappointed. The hatch
clinked open. Both of us jumped down twenty feet. On my
belt, tiny jets switched on, slowing my descent. Within seconds all the jets turned off and we ended up in waist-high
grass and, hiked. I wiped the sweat off my neck. "It's hot."

"One hundred twenty degrees Fahrenheit."

To our left, on branches, a few purple cockroaches, species
that were eight inches long, hissed.

I grimaced.

On nearby leaves, hundreds of orange ants, all of them four
inches long, marched single file, bound for someplace else.

I said, "This area is disgusting."

Eve glanced in several directions, a blank expression on her
face. A cockroach landed on her left wrist and raced up it, mucus dripping off its jaw. A particle beam shot out of her collar,
creating a barely audible noise. The beam sliced the insect in
half, rolling off her arm, screeching, *Ooot*.

"Was that insect dangerous?"

"Its stinger injects batrachotoxins into your skin. Within twenty minutes, you end up with a severe headache. An hour later, you pass out. There is a twenty percent chance that you wake up."

"Are you immune?"

"There is a sixteen percent chance that its venom would destroy twenty percent of my bio-circuits. Taking a chance is unwise."

I exhaled, trying to relax. Before long we passed four-foot-long leaves, many of them covered by half-inch gnats, a green species with yellow legs. Not far beyond them, two lilac butterflies flapped their wings. I pointed at the butterflies. "Are any of these insects dangerous?"

CHAPTER THREE

"To the contrary."

My colleague and I slogged on, stepping over tiny flowers, and kept going.

Within minutes both of us trekked past striped leaves. Beneath them, bat-like creatures, a mauve species that were upside down, their feet hanging onto the branches, purred. I pointed at the creatures. "Are they lethal?"

"Unknown. My DNAE just scanned them. Unfortunately, this genus isn't in its archives."

I clenched my teeth, disappointed by the lack of information. Forty percent of the DNAE, short for DNA Evaluator, a wrist-mounted microscopic tool, sent out electromagnetic waves. After they returned, DNAE organized them, creating quantum probability charts. The charts would help us determine what dangerous animals, plants, insects, bacteria, or viruses we would encounter.

To our left, hidden somewhere in the jungle, a creature groaned and another cackled. At the same time, the stench of death became stronger. "What stinks?"

"Rotting worms."

"I can't see them."

"My latest DNAE probe signifies that their corpses are hidden beneath the leaves that are on our right."

I said, "Gary hasn't sent us any messages since Bright Spirit arrived."

"Correct."

"Although I've sent him twenty messages during that time, he hasn't responded. LT hasn't detected any problems. Why hasn't it?" LT, short for Line Transmission software, checked for malfunctioning telecommunication issues every two minutes.

"Excellent question. I've examined LT's variables fourteen times during that period. So far, they look normal. However, that was only a superficial examination. I'll keep checking."

"Yes, keep checking."

Within the hour, both of us reached Gary's camp, a small group of huts in the dark jungle.

He stepped out of a hut.

I sighed, then asked, "Dr. Lake, have you received any of our messages?"

He smiled. "Call me *Gary*. Corv ants told me you were coming."

I blinked, surprised. "What are you talking about?"

"Months ago, not long after my team arrived in the Disig, our contact lenses and skin-mounted nanites stopped receiving or sending any text, three-D holographic, or email messages. A few hours later, I translated twenty percent of Corv's language. They pass messages between themselves. A minute after both of you arrived, the Corv told me you were coming."

Eve commented, "Fascinating."

I said, "Gary, you have a talent for translating languages."

He smiled.

"How did you develop this skill?"

"Eleven months ago, using GC, short for Genetic Conversion software, I updated my DNA."

I paused, amazed. "I've read about scientists who have updated their DNA but haven't met anybody who improved it so much they could communicate with insects."

Gary said, "Updating it was necessary."

11

Eve asked, "Gary, if we landed sixty miles from your camp, could the Corv pass that information to you?"

"You bet. As long as you touched down eighty miles from it or less, they could pass that information to me or other members of my team."

Eve asked, "Gary, did you study languages when you were a child?"

"Yes. I studied two different languages, Aito, and Qio as a hobby."

I asked, "Gary, do you know why we're here?"

"No. Why?"

I answered, "Nen Pharmaceuticals and GSA want to send a spacecraft to Heja because fourteen plants on it can be used to cure eight types of cancer. We'll pay you fifty M to be part of the crew."

Gary said, "Your offer is great. Although my current project isn't finished, the money you just promised to give me makes it possible to pay my crew enough so that they can work on this project six months longer. Dr. Venus Morton and I will accompany you."

I nodded.

Venus, an orange Qio humanoid woman, six-foot-tall, slender, stepped out of another hut. "I heard that."

Eve asked, "Venus . . . should we address you as Venus or Dr. Morton?"

"Venus."

I said, "My next step is interviewing Dr. Mark Philips."

CHAPTER FOUR

Bright Spirit zoomed upward. Venus said, "I've read about Mark and his studies a few times. Sad to say, I haven't met him in person."

Eve said, "Both of you could discuss genome palindromic repeats."

Venus scowled. "Possibly."

Eve's right hand stretched until it was seven feet long. She waved it over a distant control panel. The panel moved toward her. Her hand shrank to its original size. She examined the panel.

Gary asked, "Eve, are you a TAS?"

"Affirmative."

Gary's eyes opened wider.

Venus frowned. "Several colleagues have told me about TAS. Three complained that TAS breaks down too often."

Eve said, "Eight months ago, every TAS malfunctioned twenty percent of the time. Two weeks ago, all of them, including me, were updated. As a result, we malfunction two percent of the time."

Venus said, "It should be less than two percent."

I shook my head, disappointed by Venus's comment. "Eve is reliable."

Venus scowled. "You think so. I'll be the judge of that."

I grumbled incoherently, annoyed by Venus's attitude.

Her resume appeared in my lenses. Venus was a middle child, born in the United Provinces. Her older brother played with her from time to time. Her younger brother spent most

13

of his time with other boys. Venus argued with her parents and asked them a lot of questions regarding math, plants, and vocabulary. She collected leaves, wanting to know why and when they changed colors.

She received a bachelor's and a master's in Botany. Within three years, she received her doctorate in Botany, graduating Cum Laude.

Her resume vanished and was replaced by Mark's vita. He read a lot about swamps, rivers, and oceans. He examined thousands of three-D holograms, educational tools that mentioned the symbiotic relationship between animals and plants, then wrote many papers for his high school Ecology class.

He received his bachelor's in Ecology, graduating with honors. Two years later he was awarded a master's in Ecology. For his thesis, he wrote about turbulence in plant protein folding.

Before long, he earned his doctorate in Ecology, graduating eighth in a class of ninety. Within two weeks, Hono Labs Corporation hired him because he knew a lot about the relationship between quantum mechanics and palindromic repeats.

Our ship raced downward and stopped, hovering between towering kapoks. The on-screen landing gear came out of its bottom and hit the dirt.

Venus asked, "Do we have to park here?"

I answered, "Yes."

Gary asked, "Can't we land any closer to Dr. Philip's camp?"

Eve replied, "No. It is in a denser part of the jungle. Our team will have to hike there."

Venus said, "Hiking in this area is tiresome."

Everybody stood, walked to the right, and stopped on another section of the floor. That section dropped. All of us stepped off, pushed aside neck-high weeds, and trekked forward.

Within minutes, our group passed a line of marching ants.

Venus pointed at them. "They look hideous."

Gary said, "They remind me of Gol ants. Gol attack in large numbers."

I cringed. Several ants began humming.

Venus asked, "Why are they making that noise?"

Eve said, "They could be talking to each other."

Venus said, "Possibly. However, I guess that they're making random, meaningless sounds."

I said, "Mark hasn't sent me any messages or responded to my calls. I'm not sure if he knows we're coming or why we're doing it."

Eve said, "I'm having the same problem."

Venus said, "This expedition is a mess."

Gary said, "Venus, you have a point."

In a short while, our team came upon a small group of huts, pyramid-shaped structures with carbon nanotube walls, most of them difficult to see in the dim light. A tall white male, lanky, dressed in a mottled sepia outfit, stepped out of one. He said, "You made it."

Gary asked, "Dr. Philips, did you know we were coming?"

"Of course. By the way, call me *Mark*."

Venus asked, "How did you find out?"

Mark smiled. "The kapoks told me."

Venus scowled. "What are you talking about?"

"The moment your ship landed, lupuna trees emitted a sweet odor, indicating your ship had just arrived. Nearby sabal palmettos emitted a sour aroma, reacting to the lupuna. Four other tree species responded to the lupuna and passed that information along. Within two minutes, an adjacent ficus tree emitted a lemon scent, pointing out that your ship was here."

Venus asked, "Are you kidding?"

"Not at all."

"You're lying."

Mark frowned. "Okay. Suit yourself."

Gary said, "Venus, be nice."

"Shut up. I'm being realistic."

Gary shook his head.

I asked, "Mark, do you know why I'm here?"

"Not at all."

Eve told him. "Nen Pharmaceuticals and GSA want to send a spacecraft to Heja because fourteen plants on it can be used to cure eight types of cancer. We will pay you fifty M to be part of the crew."

Mark rubbed his chin. "The salary is impressive, making it possible to pay my assistants enough so they can work on this project for eight more months. I'll go. Leaving this area is tough. Nectar in nearby jungle daffodils might prevent yellow fever."

I said, "Our next goal is to pick up Dr. Jane Rice."

After Bright Spirit took off, her resume appeared in my lenses. She, an only child, was born in Senn, a town in Joola, a country on Waan's north coast. Her father was a farmer. Her mother worked part-time in an elementary school, teaching Libo script, a computer language.

When Jane was a teenager, she built several bio-quantum computers that used photosynthesis to solve problems. One machine was so fast, she entered it in a high school physics competition and came in first place.

Jane, a straight-A student, received a bachelor's in Physics from Tolm, a university in the United Provinces. She earned a master's of ScienceMaster of Science degree in Genetics. She was awarded a doctorate in Biophysics, graduating sixteenth in a class of fifty.

Two months after receiving her diploma, the Biophysics department gave her a grant. As part of its requirements, she had to study Qon spider venom. A colleague in the Biophysics department pointed out that if a scientist used genetic scissors, they could alter the venom. As a result, it would cure two kinds of viruses.

Because Qon lived in Meno, a group of caves in Rean, a country in Afan's western hemisphere, she and her team had to go there, collect a specific amount of venom and return it to Kess' Biophysics department.

Bright Spirit touched down near the cave entrance.

Dr. Rice, an Aito humanoid with turquoise skin appeared in my lenses. She asked, "Who are you and what do you want?"

I answered, "We're headed for a moon called Heja to find plants that can be used to cure cancer. I want to interview you. You might make a great crewmember."

She frowned. "Okay. You'll have to climb down to my campsite and help me carry some of my equipment out."

I said I would.

She vanished, ending the call.

I asked, "Eve, will you help me carry Dr. Rice's belongings out of the cave?"

"Of course."

I asked, "Does anybody else want to help?"

Venus spat, "No way. I hate caves."

Gary shook his head.

Mark refused.

Eve and I entered Meno, our shoulder-mounted flashlights switched on.

Above us, on the ceiling, fourteen Qon Spiders, a foot-long species, crawled in many directions.

I cringed. "Those arachnids are ugly."

"A valid comment."

Two dropped. A particle beam came out of my knuckle, hitting them, making them screech. *Eeeet.* Without warning they plummeted and ended up on the floor, several yards from us.

Chapter Five

I asked, "Are they dead?"

"Affirmative."

My adrenaline started pumping. Both of us hiked. To our left, more Qon crawled over stalagmites. My mind raced, trying to figure out if we should kill them. "I hate this place."

"It is a dangerous location."

Within forty minutes, we reached Dr. Rice's camp, a few domes with carbon nanotube walls.

She stepped out of one, frowning. "You made it."

I wiped the sweat off my brow.

Dr. Rice asked, "Did any Qon attack you?"

Eve answered in the affirmative.

Dr. Rice said, "This is a menacing area. You have to pay attention. Far too often, the Qon sneak up on you."

I cringed. "No doubt about it."

Eve asked, "Dr. Rice, are you ready to leave?"

"Yes. Call me Jane. My assistant, Dr. Carol Endu, a post-doc student will come with me."

I blinked, surprised. "Will she accompany you to Heja?"

"Naturally."

Eve asked, "Does she know how dangerous Heja is?"

"You bet. However, she wants to improve her skills."

I sighed. "Okay." The faint sound of scratching became louder. My neck muscles tensed up in a fearful response. "Are there any Quo nearby?"

Eve said, "A valid query. Two are in the back of you."

I spun around. Both crawled toward the ceiling, their jaws twitching.

Jane said, "We should leave. I recognize those spiders. They're more aggressive than many others."

My adrenaline started pumping. Our group slogged on. A five-foot-tall humanoid woman with striped skin trekked out of the darkness.

Eve pointed at her. "Are you Dr. Carol Endu?"

"Of course."

Jane asked Carol if she heard our conversation regarding her coming with us to Heja. She remarked that she did and pointed out that she had all her belongings in her backpack.

Shortly we passed several Qon.

Carol said, "Because their jaws are open, I realize they are hungry. Keep going. Don't slow down. If we keep up the pace everybody in our group will be safe."

Eve said, "Saliva is dripping off their jaws."

Jane said, "Don't look at them. If you do, they're more likely to attack."

Eve asked, "Carol, Jane, how have you survived?"

Carol said, "It's been tough. Although I've figured out their language, a combination of high-pitched squeaks and scratching noises, four of them have bitten me."

I blenched. "You're patient."

Carol said, "Thanks. I've always loved learning new languages. It took me six weeks to understand what many of these arachnids are saying."

Eve asked, "What do they talk about?"

Carol said, "The Oal worms. The Qon and the Oal battle constantly. When the Qon wins, they devour the Oal."

Somewhere in the gloom, a faint scratching grew louder.

I recoiled.

Jane said, "Keep moving."

CHAPTER SIX

Within minutes, our crew reached the mouth of the cave, then stepped inside Bright Spirit. Eve and I entered the cockpit and sat. I waved my hand over a motion sensor. Our ship rose and sped up. "Our next goal is to pick up Ben Green."

Dr. Carol Endu's resume appeared in my lenses.

She received a bachelor's in Entomology. This professional was awarded her Master's of Science degree in Entomology. She earned her PhD., graduating eleventh in a class of ninety.

Her vita vanished and was replaced by Dr. Ben Green's educational background.

He received his bachelor's in DNA Manipulation. He was awarded his master's in Ichthyology, graduating Magna cum laude. He earned a doctorate in Biophysics, graduating ninth in a class of forty-two. This information vanished since no more was available.

Before long, our craft raced over the ocean.

Thirty minutes later, Bright Spirit slowed down, descended, and stopped, hovering over six dugout canoes. On the ship's floor, an exit hatch whirred open. I turned, jumped through the exit, dropped slowly, helped by gravity assist, a tool, and ended up in the largest canoe.

Dr. Ben Green scowled. "What are you doing here?"

I answered. "We're headed for a moon called Heja to find plants that can be used to cure cancer. If you join us, I'll pay you fifty M."

"That is a decent salary. It will help pay for this fieldwork. By the way, call me Ben." He glanced at a nearby Aito woman and told her he would return in a few weeks. Until then she was in charge.

Gravity shift pulled both of us upward and we ended up on the ship's bridge. Ben walked toward the passenger section.

I sat in the pilot's seat. The ship lurched forward, responding to my retina and accelerated. "Our next goal is to pick up Dave Johnson, a security guard."

Eve said, "He is in the Comib."

I nodded.

Venus asked, "Is the Comib on Ejj?"

"Yes."

Gary said, "A war broke out in the Comib six months ago."

Ben said, "Going there is asking for trouble."

I cringed. Dave's resume appeared in my lenses.

He received his bachelor's of Sciences degree in Battlefield Statistics. Several weeks before awarded a master's degree in Battlefield Statistics, he dropped out and joined Lonn's Army, deciding to serve his country.

CHAPTER SEVEN

Bright Spirit dropped out of the bottom of a cloud, zoomed between mountain peaks, all of them partly obscured by mist, and descended.

Eve said, "This turbulence keeps knocking us in several directions."

I recoiled. "No doubt about it."

A laser blast, coming from artillery that was on our left, barely missed our ship's nose-mounted light.

Eve said, "Somebody thinks we're the enemy."

My adrenaline pumped faster. "Yes."

Venus hollered, "Be careful."

I winced. Our force field switched on

Bullets, coming from somewhere below us, bounced off the field.

Eve said, "Although those smart bullets ricocheted off the ship, they transmitted information to the guns that sent them. There is a forty percent chance that the next bullets might break through the field."

I recoiled. "Okay. TEV One." TEV One was short for Take Evasive Action option, ranging from one to sixty. Bright Spirit jerked starboard, entered a fifty-foot wide gorge, and the port wing ripped a branch off.

Venus exclaimed, "That was too close."

I cringed. "TEV four." Our ship lurched upward, about twenty feet. Laser blasts struck the ship's belly. "Any damage?"

Eve replied, "Two landing lights were destroyed."

I drew back.

Eve said, "Bright Spirit replaced them a second ago."

I said, "She is adapting."

Eve said, "A valid statement."

"LASC," which meant Land At Specified Coordinates. The craft plummeted.

Gary exclaimed, "This is nerve-wracking."

Venus asked, "Are we going to crash?"

I said, "No, we aren't going to crash."

Venus asked, "Are you lying?"

Eve said, "Tom knows what he is doing."

Venus said, "I don't believe it. Any second we're going to smash into a gorge wall."

A laser blast struck Bright Spirit's port wingtip.

Venus exclaimed, "Wow."

CHAPTER EIGHT

Our ship touched down in an area that was surrounded by rocks. An exit hatch whirred open. I jumped through it, landed in the dirt, then hiked toward a group of men and women soldiers.

One of the women asked, "Are you a reinforcement?"

"No. I'm looking for Dave Johnson."

She pointed to the left at a man who was twenty feet away, in a shallow foxhole. "That's him."

"Thanks." Bullets whizzed past my hips. I dropped to the ground and crawled. As gunshots rang out, I reached the foxhole.

Dave turned toward me. "Who are you?"

I answered, "My name is Tom Smith. My team is headed for a moon called Heja to find plants that can be used to cure cancer. If you join us, I'll pay you fifty M."

"That is a much higher salary. With that kind of pay, it's a lot easier to provide for my wife and six kids. I'll go."

Both of us crawled toward Bright Spirit.

On our left, a soldier asked, "Johnson, where are you going?"

He answered, "With Tom."

The soldier barked, "We need you here."

"Sorry, but if I stayed here, I would die soon."

The soldier frowned. "Shit!"

We crawled while bullets struck the outer edges of our spacesuits.

Dave burst out, "Damn. That was too close."

CHAPTER NINE

I quivered. Both of us reached the ship. GA lifted both of us inside. I walked, my adrenaline pumping then sat in the pilot's seat. At the same time, my retina switched the engines from idle to active. The craft shot upward, laser blasts barely missing its nose and belly.

Eve said, "Any second, bullets might destroy our wings."

I recoiled. "Don't remind me."

Small rocks bounced off the cockpit window.

Eve said, "Fortunately, those were small, not big enough to destroy the carbon nanotube material."

Chills ran up my spine. Within seconds, my body was jerked downward by gravitational pull.

Eve said, "If the ship moves any faster, there is a twenty percent chance that many passengers, including you, will be torn apart by rapid acceleration."

I clenched my teeth.

Within minutes, Bright Spirit entered a cloud, then shot out of its top. I said, "We have to pick up Sally Lee next."

Eve said, "My last report indicates she is in Yela's northern hemisphere, fighting drug dealers. They are hiding in the Diffi Mountains."

Many drug dealers and pioneers lived on that moon, one that was close to Afan. Mountains and deserts covered most of Yela. Pioneers, who couldn't afford to buy land on Afan, set up farms. Drug dealers hid in the mountains, a desperate attempt to avoid Afan's police.

Sally Lee's resume appeared. She was born in Vaet, a country in Wann. She had an older brother. Her parents were wealthy and spent most of their time at parties or traveling. A nanny raised her and her older brother. When she was old enough, they put Sally in Oxid, a private school that was two hundred miles away from her home.

Once a year, at Christmas, she came home to visit them. During the other holidays, the only person who came to see her was her nanny.

When she was in high school, she read a lot about the Ovit War, a conflict that took place in Waan. Months before graduation, wanting to study battlefield logistics, she applied to Corle, a university in Gof, a continent that was five hundred miles west of Wann. Four years later, she received her bachelor's of Science degree in Combat Tactics, graduating near the top of her class.

A month later, wanting to serve her country, she enlisted in the Vaet Army. Within days, she met a handsome Aito male. They married five weeks later. After two years, she was honorably discharged. Needing a steady income, she applied to Derk Security and was hired.

Our ship entered Yela's outer orbit.

Eve said, "Bright Spirit's telescopes have confirmed that Sally is two miles north of Digo's peak."

I nodded.

The ship touched down between several boulders. In the near distance, somewhere outside, gunfire rang out.

Eve said, "My last scan points out there are fifteen snipers in this area. However, since all of them have SDI equipment, determining their exact location is challenging."

I remembered that SDI, Scan Dispersion equipment destroyed electrons and molecules within a probe. My stomach muscles tightened. "Trouble." I stood. The exit hatch whirred open. I jumped through it, landed in dirt, then hunched down and trekked.

Before long, I came upon three security guards, all of them hunkered down behind a boulder. Because their cloaking fields were switched on, the only things I noticed were humanoid shapes. All the shapes were filled with blinking dots. Since all the dots were similar to the adjacent area, it was hard to tell if the shapes were guards or dirt. I sent a text message to all three of the contact lenses. *Where is Field Operative Sally Lee?*

She sent me a text message.

She is me. With that higher salary, I can send both of my sons to Esa, a private school that is far from the ghetto.

Both of us crawled away.

I walked toward my seat. On my right, Sally's cloaked field shut off, revealing an Asian woman who was five feet, six inches tall, dressed in combat fatigues.

Chapter Ten

Our ship entered clouds, all of them in Heja's sky. As the engine roared louder, we reached an altitude of six thousand feet and leveled off.

Eve said, "My last photos and three-D holograms signify that this ocean, called the Vasp, is filled with man-eating fish, dangerous eels, poisonous jellyfish, and other alien life forms."

I cringed. "What do you mean by alien life forms?"

"They are star or V-shaped."

"Are they predators?"

"Unknown."

"We'll land in the Opaan jungle. The plants we are looking for are similar to lilies. All of them are in a two-hundred-mile radius of our landing spot."

"Acknowledged."

Within twenty minutes Bright Spirit zoomed over a shore.

Before long it went between towering kapoks.

Eve said, "This jungle is vast, two thousand miles by three thousand miles."

"Although I know that, seeing the real thing is overwhelming."

A gigantic winged creature flew out from behind a huge tree.

I bellowed, "Look out!"

Eve said, "It's too late."

We struck the creature. Our right wing broke off. I broke into a cold sweat.

CHAPTER ELEVEN

The craft plummeted.

Eve said, "Prepare for impact."

Bright Spirit struck more trees. My left wall shattered. I shouted, "We're..." Above us, parts of the ceiling broke apart. My chair shook and shot upward. As my heart pounded, my chair struck a branch. Without warning, it lurched to the right, hit another, and veered to the left. Much to my surprise it dropped, crashed into bushes, and stopped.

While sweat poured down my face, the force field, designed to protect me, shut off. I rose, shoved bushes aside, and walked. In my field of vision, meaningless text scrolled because Personnel Location software had malfunctioned. I asked, "Can anybody hear me?"

In the far distance, a bird squawked. Two-inch-long red worms crawled over adjacent purple leaves. I blinked, surprised by their presence. Hidden in darkness, a scraping grew louder. I glanced in that direction, but only noticed dimly lit bushes.

Close behind me, a branch snapped. I recoiled, turned, and looked over my shoulder. In the near distance, a three-inch-long gold frog hopped onto a leaf. I exhaled, relieved, and hiked.

Text appeared in my lenses. *Cannot reach anybody on Afan because solar rays from nearby star, Proxima Centauri, keep destroying your lenses' TTO.*

Chills went down my spine. TTO, short for Telecommunication Tool made it possible to keep in touch with my colleagues via phone calls, emails, text messages, and three-D holograms

Several feet away, Eve pushed bushes aside and walked toward me.

"Are you injured?"

"Negative. What about you?"

"I'm fine. Let's search for the others."

"Excellent idea."

Both of us turned and slogged on. We passed more hull fragments, all of them hard to see in the shadows.

Shortly after, both of us stopped next to Dr. Endu's corpse. The right side of her head was gone, torn off.

My stomach churned. "We can't help her. My TTO is broken"

"So is mine."

I quivered. "When it repairs itself, I'll have to send the bad news to her family."

"Sending it to them is a valid idea."

"Because of airborne bacteria, there is a twenty-five percent chance that it will repair itself."

I sighed. "Can you repair TTO?"

"After a thorough diagnostic, a process that will take three weeks, there is a forty percent chance that my internal nanites can repair it."

I clenched my teeth. "Let's keep going."

Ten minutes later, we came upon Gary, who was sitting in a partly damaged chair. I told him about Dr. Endu.

He cringed, then lifted his right arm, one that was covered by a semi-transparent bandage.

Eve asked, "Is the wound serious?"

Gary frowned. "If the medication works, it should heal in a week or so."

"Have nanites in the bandage injected antibiotics?"

Gary sighed. "Indeed. However, a few minutes ago, my DNAE indicated that the air is filled with alien streptococcus and mutated viruses. The viruses could be filled with carcinogens."

I blanched. "Gary, have you seen the others?"

"Nope. Repairing this wound was my first priority. I didn't want to bleed to death."

Eve's DNAE clicked three times, sorting algorithms.

I said, "It's time to search for the rest of the passengers."

Eve remarked, "I'll help."

My colleague and I marched.

Eventually, we came upon Venus.

She said. "My right toe has been crushed, but my suit put a robotic covering over it. I can walk slowly. It will take about two weeks for the nanites and antibiotics to heal this injury. Damn, it hurts."

I shuddered. "Okay. Eve, let's keep searching for the others."

"Yes sir."

We trudged on and passed more chunks. Between several, a group of five-inch long orange worms hissed.

I cringed. "Eve, my DNAE's database is limited, not offering any information regarding these creatures. Are these worms poisonous?"

"There is mutated cholera on the surface of their skin. If you touch it, you get a headache in twenty minutes. There is a forty percent chance that you will pass out after that."

"Do you wake up after passing out?"

"There is a fifteen percent chance that you will wake up."

I grimaced. Both of us continued onward.

Before long we reached Mark.

He sighed. "My left knee is broken. My suit placed a robotic shield over it and my lower leg. In three weeks, nanites and antibiotics will mend this. In the meantime, I have to hike slowly."

Eve said, "Hopefully the mending process will be painless."

Mark offered a brief smile.

I said, "Let's search for the others." Both of us resumed our journey.

In a moment we came upon Sally's corpse. Sticking out of her chest was a huge branch, one that had ripped her heart and internal organs to pieces. Her eyes and mouth were open.

I quivered. "When we re-establish communications with Afan, I'll have to give her husband the bad news."

Eve's DNAE whirred, parsing archives. "She was a decent colleague. Her death was and is an unwelcome event."

"It's a good thing her death doesn't upset you."

"Why do you say that?"

"Sometimes the stench of death along with the gruesome sight of these former friends make it hard for me to concentrate."

Eve glanced at me, her silver pupils turning gold.

"Why are your eyes changing colors?"

"They're photographing and scanning this area, including every corpse and every passenger who survived. If a doctor or an important official from Afan asks me, you, or any member of this crew about this accident, I can export photographs, three-D holograms, text, and information regarding the cause of death into their lenses."

"Have you been doing this for several minutes?"

"During and after the crash."

"Good idea."

We trekked.

Before long, we reached Dave. On his forehead, was a bandage. Nanites came out of the bandage, then sutured deep cuts.

He said, "My wound will heal in five days."

I nodded. Ninety percent of the time, the bandage's software sent messages into a patient's field of vision, telling him or her when the injury would heal.

Eve said, "Dave, be careful. The air is filled with lethal microorganisms."

He glowered. "Thanks for the warning."

Eve and I tramped on.

We came upon Jane who was looking at the bandage on her shoulder.

I cringed. "Is the wound serious?"

She looked at me, scowling. "It's a deep laceration. It will heal in four days. However, it's painful." She bit her lip. "Although the nanites should have injected morphine into the wound, they didn't. For some unknown reason, they failed."

Eve said, "I'm sorry to hear they malfunctioned."

Both of us slogged on.

Within minutes we halted near Gary.

His left eye had been replaced with a robotic prosthesis.

I blinked, stunned. "It's too bad that you were injured."

His jaw muscles tightened. "Tell me about it. Although this new eye is silver, it looks fake. Its molecules will repaint it so it resembles my other eye."

Eve asked, "Is the vision in your artificial eye twenty percent?"

His left shoulder twitched. "No, it's somewhat blurred. With luck, it will be better soon. I've read about this topic. Sixty percent of the time, normal vision is restored. We'll see how it goes."

Behind towering kapoks, a creature howled.

Gary trembled. "Whatever made that noise must be huge."

I cringed. "At this point, it's obvious that our first priority is to return to Afan. Let's forget about searching for those medicinal plants."

Mark frowned. "Adjacent kapoks' scents indicate that we're in great danger."

Venus stepped over a chunk. "That sounds foolish."

"Mark, are you telling me they're smart enough to notice any threat?"

"Of course. They've created eight thousand types of odors, a language."

Eve asked, "What do you mean by great danger?"

Mark replied, "A beast surrounding trees call a Balor is coming this way. Will arrive in about five minutes."

My neck tingled in a shocked reaction. "Is it a man-eater?"

"No doubt about it. The fifteen-foot long creature bites its prey's body in half—"

Venus said, "This sounds unusual like you made it up."

"My guess, based on nine years of experience in the field, is that the threat is real, not made up."

Venus shook her head. "I can't hear the beast."

Mark said, "Several kapoks just told me it's quiet. You won't hear it until a second or so before it strikes."

I said, "Let's stand close, our backs touching. That will make it harder for the beast to sneak upon us."

Dave walked toward us. "I think we should leave before it arrives."

"Leaving right now is a good idea."

Ben asked, "Where should we go?"

Mark replied, "Nearby bushes pointed out that a strangler fig grove that is half a mile north of here is safe."

Venus scowled. "Why is it safe?"

"The strangler figs emit an odor that makes the Balor sick so it avoids that area."

Venus said, "A bunch of trees scare away a predator. It sounds like a joke."

I said, "Let's go there. It's a better choice."

"I'll go there. However, traveling to that spot sounds like a waste of time."

I said, "Venus, if you wish, stay here."

"This whole area is dark and creepy. Some insects keep chirping. The noise they make scares me."

Eve said, "Those aren't insects, they're spiders."

Venus grimaced. "How big are they?"

Eve pointed at a spot. "One just crawled out from behind a bush."

Venus snapped, "It's eight inches long. It's time to go someplace else."

Ben said, "Not long before we landed, I scanned this area. There are plants on a nearby plateau. It's eighteen miles from here, due north. Using genetic scissors, the software on my wrist-mounted DE can turn one tree's branches into a spacecraft engine. Then the DE can convert another tree's fruit into a spacecraft hull."

I blinked, surprised by Ben's remark. Some physicists used DE's, short for DNA Evaluator, to create useful machines.

Gary asked, "If this is true, how do we place the engine inside the hull."

Ben said, "At first, the engine will be small enough to carry. We have forty minutes to place it inside the hull."

Dave asked, "What happens after forty minutes?"

Ben said, "Its weight will increase to the point where none of us can carry it."

Eve said, "Another complication."

Venus said, "Somebody told me that DE's only work twenty percent of the time."

Ben scowled. "That is true. However, do you have a better plan?"

Jane said, "Venus' comment is valid. Traveling to that plateau might be a fool's errand."

Venus said, "I'm glad that somebody is listening to me."

Dave asked, "Do we have to cross rivers, canyons, or climb over any mountains to reach the plateau?"

Eve said, "We have to cross a river, hike through dense jungle, climb over a pass, and scale the plateau's cliff to reach it.'

Venus asked, "How high are its cliffs?"

Eve said, "Three thousand feet."

Dave asked, "Are the cliffs steep?"

Eve said, "Affirmative."

Jane asked, "Are there any easy routes? I don't want to fall off."

Eve said, "There is one. It's on the east side."

I said, "Let's head for the plateau."

Venus spat, "Shit."

Jane sighed.

Ben clenched his teeth. "How much food do we have left?"

I said, "We have enough wafers to last for two days."

Gary said, "I know how to live off the land. We can eat wild legumes, berries, and fruit."

Dave said, "Searching for our next meal terrifies me."

Gary's brow tightened. "It has to be done."

Jane said, "Unfortunately, Gary is correct."

I said, "We'll search for food soon."

Venus wiped the sweat off her neck. "It's hot."

Mark said, "The heat makes me tired."

A three-D hologram of the plateau, a mapping tool that was six feet high, three feet wide, appeared in front of Eve.

I asked, "Who wants to stay here?"

Mark said, "Not me."

I asked, worried, "Eve, how accurate is your hologram?"

"Forty percent."

Venus said, "Those are shitty odds."

Mark said, "Forty percent is better than twenty percent."

Venus said, "I don't like the idea of hiking through this dangerous jungle, but staying here, being alone terrifies me."

I said, "Let's go."

Everybody tramped on.

Before long, an eleven-foot long creature with gigantic teeth jumped out from behind a thicket. It growled, then moved closer.

I recoiled.

Gary said, "Adjacent gnats communicate with each other by flapping their wings at different speeds."

Eve asked, "Do they use the sound made by their flapping wings to communicate?"

"They do. Two just told me that if this beast was hungry it would tear everybody apart and devour us."

Venus burst out, "Damn!"

Jane asked, "Do the gnats assume that you understand them?"

Gary said, "I'm not sure."

Ben crossed both arms over his chest.

Gary said, "However since it finished a meal a few minutes ago, it will ignore us." The beast changed direction, crept away, and vanished in the shadows.

Mark asked, "Gary, did you make that up?"

"No. Why would you say that?"

Mark said, "You translated the gnat's language quickly. Several naturalists have told me that it takes weeks, months, or years to decipher an insect's language."

Gary scowled. "These gnats use a language that is similar to a Govay mosquito—the one that roams two of Ejj's jungles."

Mark said, "I haven't been to Ejj."

I remembered that Ejj, one of Afan's moons, was sparsely

populated. Because jungles, rugged mountains, and deserts covered most of its continents, only a few hundred humans and Aito humanoids moved there.

Jane said, "I haven't been to Ejj, either, however, Mark has a point. Gary, you could have assumed that these gnats were saying one thing. However, they might have said something else."

Gary said, "I'm experienced. I know what I'm talking about. If you wish to ignore my warnings, go right ahead. Unfortunately, if you don't pay attention to them and end up getting hurt, don't blame me."

Jane glared at him. "I won't blame you."

I said, "Let's keep going. I want to reach an open space and set up camp before dusk."

Venus clenched her teeth.

The others grumbled and our group slogged on.

Before long, we hiked between towering vines. About fifteen feet away, several winged scorpions, all about four feet long touched down.

My skin prickled with terror. "Eve, is their venom lethal?"

"It is filled with neurotoxins. If they sting you, you get a fever. Two hours later, you die."

Venus said, "Oh my god."

Adjacent vines sprayed seeds. In a moment several of the winged intruders spat. Much to my surprise all of them rose and flew away.

Dave said, "Wow, they left."

Jane asked, "Did the seeds scare them away?"

Mark said, "It looks that way to me."

Venus said, "It could have been something else. Seeds aren't scary."

Ben asked, "If the seeds didn't scare them away, what did?"

Venus asked, "Ben, why are you arguing with me?"

"I'm not arguing. I want you to consider more options."

I said, "Let's keep moving. Hopefully, those winged creatures won't come back."

Gary said, "Those winged creatures call themselves the Sern."

Venus frowned. "Are you kidding?"

Gary scowled. "No."

Venus asked, "When did you figure that out?"

"A second before they took off, one of them announced that they, the Sern, would be watching us."

Ben asked, "What did they mean by watching us?"

Gary said, "I'm not sure. That was the only thing one of them said."

Dave said, "They must have said something else."

Gary said, "They didn't."

Eve said, "Gary, you are a keen observer."

"Thanks."

Venus asked, "Eve, are you sure that his observations are accurate?"

"Judging by his experience and databases, I'm eighty percent sure."

Venus scowled.

Dave said, "Venus, noticing that angry expression on your face, you have doubts about Eve's analysis."

"Mind your own business."

Dave sighed.

Mark said, "These latest seed's movement indicates that a predator that is on our left, about ninety yards from this spot, is coming this way."

Venus said, "You can't use seeds to determine that."

Jane said, "Venus might have a point. They're seeds, nothing more."

Dave said, "I have mixed feelings about using seeds as a

warning."

I said, "Let's go to the right. I agree with Mark's suggestion."

Gary asked, "Eve, can your DNAE offer any information that will back up Mark's suggestion?"

"Not at this time. It needs more recordings, probes, and three-D holographic photographs."

I said, "Keep up the pace, don't slow down."

Venus glared at me.

Jane scowled.

Gary's brow tightened in concentration.

Dave clenched his teeth.

Ben paused, blinking, then wiped sweat off his chin.

A small three-D holographic map of this area appeared above Eve's wrist. She looked at it, a blank expression on her face.

Our group departed. On our left, hidden behind lupunas, trees that blocked out most of the sky, a crunching grew louder.

I recoiled and pointed in that direction. "What made that noise?"

Mark said, "A huicungo odor signals that a two-inch-long lizard, a harmless scavenger, made it."

Venus asked, "You're using odors as a reference?"

Mark said, "Of course. They're a good source of information."

Venus said, "That is ridiculous."

Jane remarked, "Using odors. Interesting."

Venus asked, "Jane, are you telling me that using odors is a good idea?"

"For the time being, it seems like a good one."

Venus said, "I'm surrounded by fools."

Dave blinked.

Ben, a sour look on his face, shrugged.

Gary scowled but didn't say anything.

A two-foot by three-foot DNAE screen appeared above Eve's wrist. She examined it, a blank expression on her face.

Our group tramped on.

At dusk, we reached an open space. I said, "Let's camp here."

Eve said, "I'll stand guard for the entire night."

Gary asked, "Eve, don't you need to shut down every night so that your batteries can recharge?"

"To the contrary. I can operate for several days without re-charging."

Gary said, "Impressive."

"I'm an updated model."

Gary said, "My hut won't enlarge. I'll have to use my sleeping bag."

Everybody else said his or her huts weren't functioning. They would have to use their sleeping bags.

Venus said, "What a fucking mess."

Somebody tapped me on the shoulder. I opened my eyes and sat up.

Beneath a night sky, Eve pointed at nearby ficus trees. "A creature is hiding behind those. It's making a soft hooting noise."

My adrenaline started pumping. "Can't your DNAE tell what it is?"

"For undetermined reasons, it cannot." A beam of light, coming from her eyes, illuminated the trees.

"Let's wake up Mark. Hopefully, he can use seeds or odors to ID the creature."

She nodded, walked, and touched his arm. He clenched his teeth and told him what was going on.

He rose to his feet. "A sour odor from an adjacent wimba

tree indicates that an eleven feet long predator that calls itself a Hunig is stalking us. If the Hunig is similar to a Blos, a carnivore that roams the Yope, a jungle in Xan, a continent in Ejj's southern hemisphere, chances are the Hunig won't attack. The Blos usually strikes prey that is weak or asleep."

I cringed.

Mark recoiled. "Lupuna seeds presence signifies that the Hunig is circling our campsite, waiting for the right moment to strike."

CHAPTER TWELVE

I lifted my right arm, prepared to use my half-inch long knuckle-mounted blaster—equipment that would fire one-sixteen of an inch in diameter carbon nanotube bullets.

Eve's half an inch long wrist-mounted molecular disruptor hummed. This weapon was designed to tear apart hundreds of the creature's molecules. As a result, four-inch in diameter parts of the area that it struck would disintegrate.

Two inches above Mark's left hand, a floating 2-D hologram, part of his laser blaster's scope, enlarged until it was eight inches in diameter. He whispered, "My scope's infrared sensor and motion detector can't perceive the beast."

My skin tingled in a shocked reaction.

Eve said, "My disrupter's motion-sensitive recognizer can only detect several mosquitos, not the beast."

Mark whispered, "The beast is still circling us."

I clenched my teeth.

Venus asked, "Why are you guys awake? It's past midnight."

I answered, "A Hunig is close by, ready to strike."

Venus said, "I don't hear anything. You guys are too paranoid. I'm going back to sleep."

I banged my teeth together, frustrated by her ignorant comment. About nine feet away, behind a dimly lit shiringas tree's leaves, a dark claw, barely noticeable, brushed against one of them. I aimed my weapon in that direction. Without warning, the creature rushed toward Gary's sleeping bag.

CHAPTER THIRTEEN

It slashed Gary's sleeping bag. He screamed, "Help!" Eve's disrupter hummed louder.

The predator shrieked. *Eeeeo.* Then it spun around and dashed toward me. I fired. *Eeeo.* It turned and sprinted into the jungle.

I rushed over to Gary, his sleeping bag opened. On his lower right leg, blood gushed out.

Eve arrived, sprayed a transparent bandage onto the injury and the bleeding stopped. Inside the bandage, nanites began suturing the wound.

"It should heal in five hours."

A wire came out of Gary's Hip-Mounted Protector, a half an inch in diameter disk, and went down his lower leg. At the same time, the wire expanded, creating a protective outer leg that would allow Gary to walk until the wound healed.

Gary sighed. "I'm glad that my HMP works."

I nodded. Many humans and Aito humanoids used this medical tool.

At dawn, everybody slogged on.

Venus said, "We're low on food. Damn it. Tom, you need to be more organized."

My back muscles tensed up.

Eve said, "He is doing the best he can."

Venus said, "Eve, your excuses won't cut it. Tom fucked up. I should be in charge."

I clenched my teeth, insulted. "Does anybody else want her

to be in charge?"

Gary said, "Venus, although you are a brilliant scientist, Tom should lead."

Venus said, "You're no help."

Jane said, "Never."

Everybody said they agreed with Jane.

Venus said, "You're a bunch of fools."

Before long, our group passed thorn trees.

Jane pointed at them. "There are a lot of berries on their branches."

Eve said, "My recent scan confirms that the berries are poisonous."

Gary seized a couple of them.

Venus asked, "Why did you pick those?"

Gary replied, "My genetic scissors might be able to cut a few of their exons. After they replace them with other exons, the berry could be edible."

Jane asked, "Really?"

"We'll see."

Venus shook her head. "Many botanists have tried that. Their success rate was about eleven percent."

Ben said, "We have to try. Our options are limited."

Venus said, "You're a bunch of silly dreamers. It's better to try something else."

Jane asked, "Venus, what else should we try?"

"Why are you arguing with me?"

"I'm not arguing. I want you to consider other possibilities."

Venus said, "You need to be more realistic. Listen to yourself. You sound like a fool."

Ben said, "Venus, you need to be more flexible."

"You're as foolish as Jane."

Ben shook his head.

Jane frowned.

Within the hour, our group came upon a river. I shuddered. "Those rapids are dangerous."

Venus put both hands on her hips. "Are you fucking kidding me? If we cross this everybody will drown."

Ben sucked in air through clenched teeth.

I asked, "Eve, do you have a TEB?" TEB, short for Temporary Bridges, helped explorers and others cross-rivers and gorges. When needed, this wrist-mounted tool, one that was an inch long, expanded. Its maximum length was eighty feet.

"Unfortunately, the crash destroyed mine."

Jane said, "This is going to be rough."

Venus said, "Another fucking problem."

One-sixteenth of an-inch long kayaks popped out of our wrists, landed in dirt and expanded until they were fifteen feet long. The entire group put them on the shore, grabbed side-mounted paddles, and climbed inside the boats. Rear-mounted engines switched on. All the watercraft lurched forward. A wave struck the bow. As my adrenaline pumped, my kayak jerked to the left and raced downriver.

Jane yelled, "Tom . . ."

I announced, "I can barely hear you." My boat zoomed past a boulder. As my heart pounded in fear, I stuck my paddle in the water, trying to steer to the right. My watercraft sped up, out of control.

CHAPTER FOURTEEN

On the starboard side, the kayak's sixteen of an inch-long jet-powered engine roared. The bow jerked to the left. On the boat's rear port side, another engine boomed. The watercraft lurched forward, still racing downstream. Without warning, its bottom struck a rock. The kayak tipped over and I fell out. A wave struck my face. I coughed, reached out, grabbed a handle, and climbed inside the boat.

The watercraft jerked into an upright position, lifting me out of the water. Much to my surprise, it shot forward, struck a floating branch, and jerked to the left. As my heart continued to pound, the kayak went over white water, shaking.

Within seconds, the boat swerved starboard, then reached the shore. I climbed out and walked. At the same time, my boat shrank until it was an inch long, once again to a sixteenth of an inch in diameter. I placed it on my sleeve, took a few steps, exhausted, and turned, then sat as sweat poured down my neck.

I took a deep breath, gathering my strength. Between foamy waves, a kayak without anybody in it zoomed by. I cringed. Had everybody else been swept away? I glanced to the left, but only noticed the river, not the rest of the crew. I looked in the opposite direction, and my body tensed in horror. Halfway across the water, a branch struck a boulder.

I rose to my feet, peered to the left, and only spotting trees and boulders. I hiked in that direction, went between boulders, and kept going.

I came upon Jane, the front end of her kayak ripped to pieces.

She wiped the dirt off her chin. "My boat's nanites were designed to repair that section. Unfortunately, they won't. They might have been washed away by the current."

My shoulder muscles tightened in fright. "Those nanites have been tested in the field thirty-nine times. This is the first time they have failed."

She glowered. "Tell me about it."

"You're shaking like a leaf."

She nodded.

"Are you injured?"

"No, just shocked by their failure. This kayak is supposed to be the best that money can buy."

"My TTO is still broken. How about yours?"

"Alert text indicates that it has only repaired six of its eighteen bio-circuits. The rest of them are crushed, useless. Hopefully, TTO's nanites can restore them."

I took a deep breath, trying to relax. "Let's search for the others."

Her boat shrank like mine—one inch long, a sixteenth of an inch in diameter. She placed it on her sleeve, and we tramped on.

After a while, as we passed weeds and a wimba grove, both of us reached Ben. Several yards away, the port side of his kayak had been torn off.

He stood, teeth clenched, then said, "It's good to see you. I was worried that everybody else drowned."

Jane asked, "Are you hurt?"

He quivered. "There was a deep cut on my ankle. Fortunately, nanites have sutured the wound and have applied antibiotics. Genetic scissors cut some exons and replaced them with better DNA strands. As a result, the injury will heal faster."

I asked, "Why are you shaking?"

"The wound still hurts."

Jane asked, "When will the pain stop?"

Ben clenched his teeth and said, "My best guess is a couple of hours from now."

I said, "Normally, after the better DNA strands are in place, the pain stops."

Ben wiped the sweat off his chin. "Yes, normally. As you can tell, this is unusual. My contact lens' graphs verified that there is a twenty percent chance that alien viruses have destroyed too many of the best DNA strands."

Jane asked, "How many?"

Ben said, "My lens' GEX hasn't finished examining the strands."

Many humans and members of the Aito race referred to Genome Examination software as GEX. I asked, "When will your lens come up with an answer?"

"I'm not sure."

Jane said, "That is bad news. GEX was designed to answer that question is four minutes or less."

Ben sighed. "It's true. However, the only thing I can do is wait."

I said, "Let's search for the others."

Ben's kayak shrank. He placed it on his sleeve.

Within the hour we found everybody but Venus.

I said, "We must keep looking."

After passing several walking palms our group entered a shiringas grove.

Jane said, "It's dark, hard to see anything."

Mark said, "This area stinks."

Eve commented, "A valid complaint."

About twenty feet away, a dimly lit humanoid figure was on the ground, it's back against a tree. I pointed at the figure. "Is that Venus?"

CHAPTER FIFTEEN

All of us stopped. It *was* Venus. She was covered from head to toe by a clear substance. Because it was tightly wrapped around her, she couldn't move or speak.

I recoiled. "Your mouth is covered by this stuff."

She blinked.

A laser beam came out of Eve's wrist and cut some of the substance off.

Venus announced, "Thanks."

I asked, "How did you end up like this?"

"After reaching shore, I crawled a few feet. Something growled and so glanced in that direction. A creature with two legs ran toward me, spitting. Then I passed out. I woke up a few minutes ago."

Mark asked, "How tall was the creature?"

"There wasn't enough light. I didn't get a good look at it."

Eve sliced the rest of the substance off. "This is dried saliva."

Ben said, "Sickening. An alien beast ties its victims up with dried spit."

Gary blanched.

Mark cringed.

I said, "Let's keep going, head for the plateau. I want to reach an area that is closer to it before dusk."

Everybody else agreed.

About twenty minutes later after our group left the grove, we hiked between towering ferns. A branch snapped. I asked,

"Is something following us?"

Eve said, "My DNAE just confirmed that a nine-foot-tall species is."

Mark asked, "Can you provide more information?"

"Unfortunately, that is impossible."

Venus scowled. "Why not?"

"Airborne seeds are partly blocking the probes."

Venus scowled. "Tom, why did you pick this area to hike through?"

My back muscles tightened in frustration. "It's the shortest route."

Venus said, "I'm smart, so I should be leading this group."

Jane said, "Tom is capable."

Venus asked, "Who asked you?"

Jane said, "I have a right to speak. Besides, you have a lousy attitude. You didn't thank Eve when she cut you loose."

Venus grumbled incoherently.

On the opposite side of Jane, Mark said, "A sweet odor proves that a creature is twenty feet behind us, hiding behind ferns."

Jane asked, "Does the odor indicate that the creature is a predator?"

Mark said, "It only shows the creature's location, nothing more."

Gary said, "Several nearby worm's stench proves that the creature, a species that calls itself a Notak, is waiting until sundown. Then it will strike."

Venus said, "Worms are stupid, so they won't provide that kind of information."

My back muscles tightened in irritation. "Gary knows a lot about worms and other creatures. You can learn a lot by listening to him."

Venus scowled.

At dusk, the entire crew halted at a clearing, an area surrounded by neck-high weeds. I said, "This isn't perfect, but it's the safest spot I've seen all day."

Venus glowered.

Gary sighed.

Mark, a fatigued expression on his face, scratched his chin.

A chair popped out of Jane's wrist. It expanded and she sat in it.

Eve said, "I want to stand guard for the night. However, I must go into sleep mode for six hours so that software can repair several of my contaminated bio-circuit boards."

I shuddered. "Did airborne viruses or bacteria contaminate them?"

"At this point, determining that is difficult. There is a forty percent likelihood that the software, an application called Evaluator can answer your question after I wake up."

My mind raced, trying to figure out what to do if airborne viruses or bacteria destroyed Eve. "I'll stand watch."

Jane scowled. "Tom, can you stay awake the entire night?"

"I think so. Why do you ask?"

"You look tired. Every few minutes, you close your eyes shut."

"Okay, relieve me four hours after midnight."

About half an hour before midnight, a distant thrashing, barely noticeable, grew louder. I blinked, worried. Approximately sixteen feet above me, a three-foot-long indigo bat-shape, a silhouette that was difficult to see because it was the same color as the sky, swooped down. As my adrenaline pumped, the shape whizzed by, entered the jungle, and vanished, hidden in the shadows.

Twenty minutes later, I heard a faraway whooping and cringed. Was it coming from my left, or right? It was hard to tell since the noise only lasted a few seconds.

Within a short amount of time, I glanced to the left. Twenty feet away, a line of arrow-shaped insects, all about three inches along, crawled out of a hole and marched toward the jungle. While chills went down my spine, all of them went behind waist-high grass and disappeared, hidden by it.

Jane tapped my right shoulder. I blinked.
She whispered, "You fell asleep."
"Sorry."
"Did I miss anything?"
I talked about the recent events.
"Shit, this is a busy place. One of those could have attacked us."
"Maybe. On the other hand, they didn't. They could have been harmless."
She glared at me.
I sighed, not sure what to say. "It's time for me to sleep."
She frowned. "Okay."

At dawn, Venus said, "Tom, you should have woken everybody up when that creature flew overhead."
I shook my head, frustrated by her comment.
Eve said, "It's difficult for Tom to make the best decision. He was dealing with an alien creature that was unlike any we have encountered before."
Mark said, "Several fragrant odors, created by huicungo trees corroborate that the winged creature was an herbivore."
Venus said, "There you go, making ridiculous comments about odors made by trees."
Mark frowned. "My comments are based on years of experience."
Venus glared at him.
I said, "It's time to resume the journey."

Shortly, after passing towering ferns, Mark said, "There are bushes ahead. The berries on them are edible."

Gary remarked, "That is great. I'm hungry."

Venus shrugged.

Ben commented, "My DNAE just detected a six-foot-high creature."

I blinked. "Is it on our left, or right?"

Ben remarked, "It was on our right, about eighty feet away. However, now it's gone."

Eve said, "Fascinating. My DNAE never detected it."

Gary said, "I heard it whisper."

Jane asked, "Whisper?"

"Yes."

"Was it speaking?"

"It was."

Mark asked, "What did it say?"

Gary said, "Something about a Gono."

Ben asked, "What is a Gono?"

"I don't know. That was all it said."

Venus announced, "Some creatures use different pitches to communicate. Others make noises that provide limited information."

Ben asked, "What do you mean by limited?"

Venus replied, "When the Reta worms squeak, they are only announcing their position in the jungle, nothing more."

Eve asked, "Where do Reta worms live?"

Venus said, "In the Ollan Jungle."

"The Ollan in the Republic of Goln."

"Your memory is impressive."

Eve nodded.

My contact lenses remained blank, not providing any information regarding the Reta.

Gary scowled. "Venus, you told me that Corv and other

creature's sounds were just as sophisticated as English, Chinese, Aito, or other languages."

"I used to believe that."

Gary asked, "What do you mean, *used to*?"

She glared at him. "I assumed that the different pitches, varying tempos, and the endless variety of noises made by Yame slugs and Qofo Beetles indicated that these creatures shared a lot of complex information."

Gary asked, "What do you mean by *complex information*?"

"The location of food, the nutritional value of it, family history, politics, wishes, hopes, dreams."

Eve asked, "What were the Yame and Qofo saying?"

Venus replied, "Most of the time they were saying they found some food, or they wanted a mate, nothing too complex."

Gary asked, "Do you assume that every insect or creature in the jungle is as simple-minded as the Yame or Qofo?"

Venus glowered. "For the time being, yes, I assume that. We want to believe that these species are smarter than they are."

Gary said, "You need to study the sounds and body language made by other species, not assume they are as simple-minded as the Yame or Qofo. The Nool bird's songs indicate directions, hopes, dreams, food location, and other valuable information."

Venus said, "I don't know much about the Nool. However, my guess is that anybody who believes their songs convey a lot of information is dreaming because they want to believe that the Nool are smarter than they really are."

Gary gnashed his teeth.

Venus said, "Judging by that expression on your face, you don't like my last statement."

Gary mumbled incoherently and walked away.

Venus announced, "Gary, if you think about what I just

said, you will realize it makes sense."

Eve said, "Venus, there are billions of species in this galaxy. Your statement regarding these creature's simple-mindedness could be premature."

"You're just a robot. Androids are flawed." She stomped off.

I sighed. "That didn't go well."

Ben shrugged.

Not far beyond him, Jane sucked in air through clenched teeth.

Mark cleared his throat. "It looks like our honeymoon period is over."

I said, "Despite our differences, we have to make it to the plateau."

Jane sighed. "We're low on food."

Eve said, "I'll look for some."

My mind sped up, trying to think of the best places to search. "Gary, has any nearby creatures mentioned any edible plants that are close by?"

He glowered. "No."

Eve asked, "Mark, have plants talked about any edible berries, legumes, or other flora that are a short walk from here?"

He blinked. "Not as far as I know."

I said, "Eve, let's go." My colleague and I then departed.

In no time, both of us passed towering lupuna. On their leaves, a few six-inch-long gold frogs blew bubbles. Somewhere far beyond towering strangler figs, an animal called out. *Oooowet.*

I quivered. "What made that noise?"

Eve said, "My DNAE probe confirms that a winged chameleon did. Unfortunately, it's unlike any species on my database."

I blinked, surprised. "Is it dangerous?"

"That is yet to be determined."

A star-shaped creature, three feet long, the same color as fucus bark, jumped off a nearby branch and ended up on a leaf.

My neck tensed up. "Is that creature lethal?"

"Unknown. It is the same genus as the Keop, an herbivore that roams the Disig Jungle."

"I haven't been to the Disig."

Eve replied, "I've only watched three-D holograms of explorers who have hiked through it."

"Is the Disig as dark as this?"

"It is not."

We came upon purple berries. I asked, "Are these edible?"

"Affirmative. However, if you eat them, you may hear scratching noises, and experience hallucinations."

"I'm hungry, will put up with the hallucinations."

"Very well."

Our chest-mounted pouches opened, and we stuffed several pounds of berries in them. After finishing we hiked.

Before long, pollen fell from the sky. I blinked, surprised. "Where is this stuff coming from? It's all over my arms and hands."

Eve answered, "Unknown."

"Is it lethal?"

"Unknown."

"Is it seeds, pollen, or what?"

"Seeds."

"Are they edible?"

"Difficult to ascertain. Wait a second. A DNAE evaluation has determined that if you inhale too many of these seeds, they block your sinuses and you end up with a severe headache."

I shoved the seeds off.

Eve pointed at several three-foot-tall bushes. "Their roots are edible. Although they taste like dirt, you can live on them."

Both of us ripped several out and tore off the roots. Our backpacks moved until they were over our chests. Within seconds, they opened. We filled them up. They closed and returned to their original position. Both of us trekked, retracing our steps.

When we reached camp, I asked, "How is everybody doing?"

Jane scowled. "Everybody's TTO is still broken. As a result, none of us contacted you regarding Mark's disappearance."

I quivered. "When did he vanish?"

Dave glowered. "About fifteen minutes after both of you took off, he said he was going to use the bathroom, would return soon."

Venus clenched her teeth. "He never came back."

Eve asked, "Did anybody search for him?"

Venus snapped, "Of course. That is a stupid question."

Gary said, "Ben and I did."

I asked, "Did you find his footprints?"

Ben said, "No."

Eve asked, "Did you call out his name?"

Gary said, "Several times. He didn't answer."

I asked, "Gary, did any insects discuss his disappearance?"

He glowered. "Not at all. Several mosquitoes buzzed in a variety of pitches, indicating that our footsteps were loud."

I said, "Let's search for him in small groups. Jane and Venus, pair up, then go north. Ben, Gary, and Dave, work together, head west. Eve and I will team up, heading east."

Everybody split up and departed.

Eve's DNAE clicked. "A creature is following us."

My back muscles tensed up. "My DNAE can't detect it and I can't see or hear the creature. Where is it?"

"It's thirty feet away, hidden behind Pallas."

"Why can't my DNAE spot it?"

"I've updated my DNAE three times in the last twelve hours. If I didn't, pollen would block its probes."

"Are the trees blocking our probes on purpose?"

"Intriguing question. Unfortunately, I can't answer your query."

I banged my teeth together, disappointed. "Why not?"

"There are many possibilities. One is that molecules in the pollen eliminate the probe's electrons. The molecules don't do this on purpose. On the other hand, the creature might be using electrical charges to cloak itself."

"When can you come up with a definite answer?"

"When my DNAE"s quantum computer has enough information."

I sighed, frustrated. "When will that be?"

"There is a forty percent chance that it can provide an accurate answer in fifty-nine minutes."

My mind sped up, trying to think of a better way to locate Mark. About thirty feet away, an eight-foot-tall creature, a biped, barely noticeable in the shadows, rushed out from behind a kapok, then went behind dangling vines, ones that were twenty feet away.

CHAPTER SIXTEEN

I recoiled then pointed in that direction. "Did you see that beast?"

"To the contrary, I was looking in the opposite direction."

I sighed, aggravated. "I'm guessing that it was a Notak. My DNAE only detected vine and weed RNA along with their genome."

Hours later, at dusk, after giving up, everybody reached camp. I asked, "Did anybody find Mark's boot prints, torn clothing, or anything else?"

Venus snapped, "Nothing."

Ben scowled. "It's as if he vanished into thin air."

Gary shook his head.

Jane said, "This is awful."

Dave said, "It's hopeless."

At dawn, the entire crew resumed the journey, bound for the plateau.

Within the hour, the group came upon a gorge. To the left, there was a natural bridge, one made of granite. I pointed at it. "Let's cross that."

Everybody marched toward it.

Venus said, "That bridge looks shaky."

A cracking grew louder. Beneath her, rocks broke apart. She looked down, a terrified expression on her face.

CHAPTER SEVENTEEN

Venus plummeted. I glanced downward. Twenty feet below me, she grabbed a branch then she screamed, "Some . . ."

Eve's left arm stretched out, moving toward Venus.

I drew back, shocked "Can you reach her?"

Eve said, "Perhaps." She grabbed Venus' outstretched hand and started pulling her up. Rocks fell off the cliff, then zipped past her shoulder.

Jane said, "Terrifying."

Ben commented, "Oh my god."

Gary shuddered. "Eve's arm is moving slowly. Will it fall apart?"

Dirt fell off the cliff and bounced off of Venus' head. She trembled.

Gary frowned. "Should we stay here? This cliff is falling apart."

Eve pulled Venus onto nearby ground.

Gary said, "Wow."

Venus took a deep breath, then coughed.

I said, "Let's hike ten feet from the cliff's edge. This bridge is the safest way to cross the gorge."

Venus glowered. "The safest?"

Eve said, "The only other bridge is fifteen miles away. We have to climb over an eleven-thousand-foot-high mountain to reach it."

Ben said, "This bridge will have to do."

Jane said, "I don't like it, but Tom and Ben are correct."

I said, "I'll go first."

Venus said, "You're a fool."

My back muscles tensed up in irritation. I started across. Underneath my boot heels, a cracking became louder.

CHAPTER EIGHTEEN

Venus shouted, "You'll never make it."
I clenched my teeth, bothered by her comment. Pebbles rolled off the bridge and plummeted. Not far from the pebbles, tiny fractures spread. Gusting wind blew dust into my eyes. I blinked, trying to get rid of the sediment. Without warning, I tripped and landed face down in the dirt.

Eve asked, "Are you injured?"

"No." I rose, then hiked on.

Before long, Eve, the last to cross, reached the other side. The entire crew trekked.

Jane said, "That was horrible."

Venus said, "Horrible is correct. We were lucky."

Ben said, "Venus, you need to be more positive."

"Mind your own business."

Jane said, "Venus, you're too pessimistic."

"Shut up."

Gary said, "Venus, you shouldn't talk to her like that."

"That's the way I am. Get used to it."

Gary frowned.

I said, "Let's keep going. We need to find an open space, a location where a Notak or another creature is less likely to attack, before dusk."

After hiking through a denser part of the jungle, a spot where most of the dimly lit bushes and dark neck-high weeds were difficult to see, we came upon a few six-foot-long umber worms. Two of them hissed.

I cringed.

Ben said, "These invertebrates stink."

Jane vomited. Within seconds, she cleared her throat and said, "The stench upset my stomach."

Eve asked, "Jane, are you sick?"

"No. I feel better now. Thanks for asking."

Eve said, "Excellent."

Hidden behind kapoks, a crunching grew louder.

I quivered.

Gary asked, "What is making that sound?"

A seven-foot-tall creature, a gray biped with huge teeth, stepped out from behind a gigantic bush.

I drew back.

CHAPTER NINETEEN

Venus yelled, "Watch out."

Dave raised his obliterator, a one-inch long knuckle mounted weapon. It crackled.

A two-inch in radius spot on the beast's neck crumbled. The animal collapsed, howling. *Oiihhh.*

Mark stepped out from behind kapoks.

Venus exclaimed, "We thought you were dead."

He blinked.

I asked, "Where were you?"

Jane said, "We spent a lot of time searching for you."

Mark glowered. "When I was heading back to camp, I spotted a Notak that had been stalking me. I fired at it, then veered to the right, went between lupuna trees, and kept going. Hours later, after guessing that the creature had stopped following me, I trekked toward camp. When I reached it, everybody had departed. So, I kept going, bound for the plateau."

I blinked. "Amazing."

Eve said, "Your survival skills are impressive."

Venus gave him a stern look.

Dave said, "Wow."

Jane remarked, "I agree with Eve's comment."

Gary smiled.

I said, "Let's keep going."

Everybody trekked on, Jane and me behind the others.

After climbing over a gloomy ridge, one covered by towering wimba, I glanced over my shoulder, wondering why I couldn't hear Jane's footsteps. There was only the jungle. "What happened to Jane?" I looked straight ahead.

Several feet away, Eve glanced in my direction. "Good query."

Gary frowned. "That is strange."

Not far beyond him, Mark scowled. "Wasn't she here a few minutes ago?"

Venus' brow tightened.

I said, "Let's search for her." The others agreed and the entire group marched, retracing our steps.

Within a short amount of time, Mark said, "Airborne kapok seeds indicate that Jane is on our left, sixty feet away, covered by branches."

Venus said, "Unbelievable."

Dave said, "I agree with Mark." The entire crew trekked in that direction.

Ben said, "There isn't much light."

I pushed waist high undergrowth aside.

We came upon piled up branches.

Ben asked, "Is she underneath those?"

Venus said, "Probably not."

Eve, Mark, and I grabbed some branches and tossed them away, the others joining in.

After removing hundreds of branches, I said, "She isn't here."

Eve pointed straight ahead, at more piled-up branches. "She could be underneath those."

I asked, "Can your DNAE detect her?"

"To the contrary."

Gary said, "Mine can't either. She is probably somewhere else."

I said, "Pull off these branches."

Venus asked, "Why should we?"

I said, "My hunch is that she is under these."

Mark sighed. "Okay."

Everybody hiked toward the piled-up branches, reached them, and started tossing them away.

Chapter Twenty

Within a few minutes, we discovered a piled-up indigo mound that was eight feet high. I touched it. "It's hard as rock."

Eve's hand turned into a circular saw and began cutting the hard substance.

Venus said, "This is a wasted effort. We should go someplace else."

As my thoughts raced, trying to figure out if Jane was nearby Eve yanked off chunks of the indigo. "This substance is hardened mucus."

I cringed.

Ben said, "Yuck, disgusting."

Gary pulled off more pieces, revealing hair. "What?"

I said, "Keep digging."

Before long, we uncovered Jane's face. Her eyes were closed.

"Jane, are you awake?"

Her eyes remained shut.

Ben asked, "Is she alive?"

I shuddered.

After tearing off all the chunks, I realized she was in a sitting position. The skin on her neck and face was red.

Eve said, "It's a good thing we found her right now. She is covered by saliva. In a few hours, it would have dissolved her skin and she would have died."

71

Gary asked, "Why is she covered with spit?"

Eve said, "A creature uses the saliva to keep its victims in one spot. After they die, it returns, and it devours them."

Mark paused, a horrified expression on his face. "Why doesn't it eat them right away?"

"My guess, based on limited information, is that it hunts constantly. Because it wasn't hungry, it stored Jane—its food. If it couldn't find another meal and is hungry, it returns to this spot and eats her."

Venus commented, "Repulsive."

I took a deep breath, trying to relax.

Mark asked, "Will Jane wake up?"

Eve said, "My last quantum probe confirms that there is a sixty percent chance she will."

A carrier came out of Eve's back. She turned. The carrier's gravitational field lifted Jane and she ended up on Eve's back.

I said, "Let's get out of here before this predator returns."

The entire group slogged on, bound for the plateau.

Within the hour as the group stepped over a stream, one that flowed between towering huicungo, Eve asked, "Tom, can you hear that sniffing?"

I blinked. "No."

Gary said, "I can't hear it either. However, a group of adjacent gnats is flapping faster. That increased speed means that a predator is close by."

I asked, "Is the predator on our right, left, or where?"

Mark said, "A scent given off by creepers indicates that a large beast is on our right, sixty yards away."

Eve asked, "Is the beast following us?"

Mark said, "The scent tells me that it is."

My shoulder muscles tensed up in a scared response.

Venus hesitated. "I don't see or hear any beast."

Mark said, "It's there."

I said, "If it comes any closer, fire."

Dave glowered.

Jane blinked.

I asked, "Jane, are you feeling better?"

"I'm . . ."

Eve said, "Her recovery is slow. A quantum graph has determined that she won't be able to say more than a word or two for a couple of days."

Dave said, "This silence is getting on my nerves. If only that beast would make some noise."

Mark said, "It's skilled, knows how to move without stepping on most leaves, branches or brushing against anything hard enough to make any noises."

Venus asked, "Mark, how would you know that?"

"Two gnats are emitting hypersonic squeaks. The sound indicates that the predator is close by."

Ben said, "I can't hear the squeaks."

Mark said, "I updated my microphone earlier today. As a result, it detected the squeaks and translated them."

Venus asked, "Detected and translated them? How could it do that so fast?"

Mark said, "The microphone's database contains eight trillion kinds of squeaks, sounds made by five million different insect species. This includes gnats, flies, hornets, wasps, bees, nona, and vela."

Ben said, "I've never heard of nona and vela."

Mark said, "They're found in Lonn's jungles."

Gary asked, "How does your microphone organize the sounds?"

Mark said, "By pitch, the length of silences between the squeaks, the duration of each squeak, the volume, the amount of bass, and the amount of treble."

Venus sighed.

Before long, our group hiked through neck-high grass. On a branch that was about fifteen feet above the ground, a two-foot-long lizard with mottled taupe skin wheezed. I pointed at it. "Is it dangerous?"

Mark said, "To the contrary. It's helping us."

Ben asked, "How is it doing that?"

"The duration of its call indicates that all of us should trek straight ahead for two hundred yards. Then we should circle around a huicungo grove."

Dave asked, "Why is this lizard helping us?"

Mark said, "Its call is a warning to other members of its species."

On Eve's back, Jane yawned.

I asked, "Jane, are you feeling better?"

"Although all my muscles ache, I *do* feel better."

Eve said, "Excellent."

Jane asked, "How did we end up here?"

I answered, "A predator kidnapped you. Then it imprisoned you in dried mucus. We set you free."

Jane drawled, "One of the last things I remember is some mist hitting my face. Then I became dizzy and passed out."

Dave asked, "Did anybody hear that whooshing noise?"

Ben frowned. "Barely. It's on our left, about sixty feet away, hidden in darkness."

I asked, "Mark, what is making that sound?"

He glowered. "Unknown."

Gary said, "Scents given off by lilacs indicate that two Sern made that sound."

I asked, "Are they going to attack us?"

"The Sern are mating, don't care what we are doing."

Venus giggled. "They're too busy fucking."

Dave glowered. "I'm glad you think it's funny."

Venus asked, "Don't you think it is?"

Dave said, "Not at all."

A few minutes later Gary said, "Nearby, airborne spores, ones coming from mold confirm my theory that our group should keep going straight ahead. If we hike to the left, a Balor that has been stalking us is more likely to strike because that area is darker than our current location."

Chills ran up my spine.

Dave said, "And since it is darker, spotting the predator before it attacks will be harder."

Gary said, "Exactly."

Venus said, "My stomach is growling. I'm starving."

I said, "When we reach a safer area, Eve and I will search for food."

Ben said, "I'm tired. A decent meal would give me more energy."

Not far above adjacent treetops, a flock of V-shaped creatures flapped their wings.

Mark pointed at them. "Eve, anybody, are they carnivores?"

Gary said, "Good question."

Venus jeered, "Gary and Mark, both of you are smart. I'm amazed that you don't know."

Mark sighed. "This is a huge jungle, a spot we haven't been to before."

Ben asked, "Mark or Gary, are the species that live here somewhat similar to those in other rain forests?"

Mark responded first. "Some are. However, only a few of their hunting practices are similar to other species. It will take time to determine if the rest of their hunting practices are the same or extremely different."

Gary added, "I agree with Mark."

At dusk, our group set up camp in an open space.

I asked, "Gary, Mark, anybody, do you want to help Eve

and I locate some food?"

Gary said, "I'm too tired."

Mark wiped sweat off his forehead. "I'm too exhausted."

The rest of the group said they needed to rest.

Eve and I hiked.

Within minutes, she halted near small thorn trees. "These are votab. Their roots are edible."

Both of us ripped several out.

Eve's right hand changed into a circular saw and cut the roots into small pieces. Our waist-mounted pouches opened, and we placed the roots in them. The pouches closed and we departed.

Eve said, "After a human consumes these roots, they hallucinate."

I blinked. "Will humans see animals that aren't there?"

"On the contrary, quantum graph evaluations, based on four thousand human central nervous system responses, indicate that humans will smell bitter and sweet odors, ones that are fake."

"That sounds harmless."

"Perhaps."

I had to ask, "What do you mean by perhaps?"

"From time to time, Jane and Aito use odors to spot dangerous beasts."

"I've heard about that. A lot of Aito use odors to find predators."

"Correct. Once she consumes these votab roots, it will be harder for her to smell beasts."

I shuddered. "We need all the help we can get in terms of noticing predators that are close by."

"Exactly."

To our left, a distant creature howled. *Ooooobboo.*

My stomach muscles tightened. "What made that noise?"

"My DNAE is offering conflicting results."

"What does that mean?"

"There is a twenty percent chance that a Balor made that sound. However, a creature that isn't in my archives might have made it."

"What kind of creature is it?"

"It's six feet long with four legs. No more information is available."

I exhaled, trying to relax. Both of us retraced our steps.

We reached camp.

Mark said, "Aphids are flapping their wings at thirty different intervals. That is a warning."

I blinked, caught off guard by his remark. "What kind of warning?"

"A creature that calls itself a Norn, a predator that camouflages itself by changing colors, will arrive soon. We must leave before it shows up."

Venus asked, "We're supposed to leave because they're flapping their wings?"

Mark glowered. "No doubt about it."

Venus spat, "It's an unrealistic warning."

Eve's DNAE hummed, organizing data.

I said, "Let's go."

Everybody but Venus departed.

Gary said, "Venus, staying here is a bad idea."

"I'll catch up with you soon."

"Venus, are you going to rest?"

"Yup."

Before long, our group slogged between towering Pallas. On their leaves, inch-long caterpillars chewed pieces of bark.

Within the hour, Eve said, "Venus hasn't caught up with

us."

Jane drawled, "She is too lazy for her own good."

I said, "Eve, let's go back for her."

"As you wish."

Mark said, "Going back for her is a lousy idea. The Norn is lethal."

I said, "She is hard to get along with. However, she is worth saving."

Gary said, "Tom, if both of you don't return, should we keep going?"

"Yes."

Eve and I left, retracing our steps.

Forty minutes later, we arrived at a dimly lit spot. Leaves shook, blown by the wind.

Eve said, "This area is quiet — too much so."

"Is that a sign?"

"A valid query. A predator is nearby."

I breathed slowly, trying not to panic.

Eve pointed upward. "Do you see that humanoid shape?"

"No."

"It's upside down, covered in leaves."

I quivered. "Now I see it."

Eve took a few steps, jumped up, and landed on a branch, then started tearing off leaves off the bottom.

"It's dark. Who or what is it?"

"It's Venus."

I cringed.

Chapter Twenty-One

Eve cut off the rest of the leaves. "Her left arm is gone, chewed off."

Chills ran up my spine. "Can you bring her down? We need to get out of here."

"An appropriate request."

Her gravity assist turned Venus until she was right side up. In one quick motion, the device placed her on Eve's back. Eve jumped down.

I asked, "Venus, can you hear me?"

Her eyes and mouth, both closed, didn't budge. On the end of her shoulder, the spot where the top of her arm was chewed off, a gray substance that had been placed on top of the bone moved down a quarter of an inch.

I pointed at the substance. "Eve, what is it?"

"My DNAE can't ID the gray matter."

"The only answer mine came up with is that this life form is unlike anything on Afan, Yela, Ejj, or Iap."

"Acknowledged. My DNAE is sorting through photos, three-D holograms, and DNA files. Bayesian statistics have determined that finding realistic answers will take anywhere from three seconds to a week."

I twitched, shocked, then opened her mouth with my hand.

On her tongue, sticky black residue seeped forward. I grabbed part of it and yanked it out.

"Her mouth is filled with a gooey substance. It's an alien mold, an organism that isn't on my archives."

"An ugly revelation."

"Yes. Let's go." Both of us slogged on. About sixteen feet away, an eight-foot-tall mound, difficult to see in the shadows, hissed.

I pointed at it, my adrenaline pumping. "Is that a creature or a pile of dirt?"

"Although my DNAE has sorted through eighteen trillion archives, it hasn't come up with a realistic answer."

My jaw muscles tightened in frustration.

Shortly after, we passed dangling vines. Venus barfed and the gooey substance ended up on her chest. Without warning, the substance began crawling downward.

I reached out, grabbed the runny material, and threw it to the ground. Tiny round creatures leaped out of it, screeching. *Eeeeooo.*

I aimed my weapon. A laser beam came out of it, hitting the creatures. *Eeeeoo.*

Eve's head, not her body, turned around. "What is occurring?"

I answered, "Venus threw up because predators were inside her stomach."

Eve said, "It's necessary to probe her stomach."

I recoiled. "Why?"

"These creatures might be in it, devouring that vital organ."

Chills ran up my spine. "How can you probe it?"

"With surgical nanites."

"Have you ever used them before?"

"This is the first time."

I cringed. "Isn't there anything else you can do?"

"Absolutely not."

"Okay. Use the nanites."

A stream of these tiny robots flew out of Eve's wrist and entered Venus' mouth.

My back muscles tensed up in a stunning reaction. "We

must hike. My guess is that the Notak is close by."

"As you wish." Her head turned until it was facing forward.

Both of us marched.

While we stepped over branches Eve remarked, "The tiny creatures crawled into Venus' stomach and cut a one-inch in diameter hole in it."

"That is horrible."

"A valid comment. On the plus side, several minutes later, the nanites obliterated all the creatures, removed them, and sewed the hole shut."

"Can she eat, not experience any pain?"

"Affirmative."

I plummeted.

CHAPTER TWENTY-TWO

As my adrenaline pumped harder, I said, "I've fallen into a hole. There are animal corpses all around me. They stink." My stomach churned, responding to the stench. "All of them are covered with dried saliva."

Above me, Eve said, "I can't see you because the hole is too far away."

"Walk toward my voice."

"A valid request."

A scratching became louder. I glanced in that direction. Several feet away, a claw lurched toward me.

I shuddered. "Hurry." A laser beam came out of my hand, then struck the claw. A beast, obscured by darkness, bellowed. *Ooooom.*

"What is going on?"

"Something is . . ."

The claw jerked toward my arm. My beam hit it again. *Oooom.*

Eve said, "It's difficult to see you."

Her outstretched hand shot downward. I grabbed it, my heart pounding. She yanked me upward.

I landed next to her.

"Something is what? Explain yourself."

"Let's get out of here."

"As you wish."

We hiked on.

Before long, my partner asked, "What attacked you?"

I answered, "A beast with claws. Because the hole was poorly lit, most of the predator was hidden in darkness."

"Your description is vague. Also, there wasn't enough time for my DNAE to scan the predator."

I exhaled, trying to relax.

"You are shaking. The experience must have been traumatic."

"Traumatic is an understatement."

Within hours, we came upon the others.

Ben asked, "Tom, what happened? You look nervous."

I replied, "I fell into a hole and a beast attacked me, then Eve pulled me out."

Gary said, "It sounds terrifying."

"It's time to head for the plateau. Staying around here is dangerous."

Everybody trudged on.

After hiking over seven ridges, we came upon a gorge.

Jane pointed to the left. "We can't cross that natural bridge. It's falling apart."

Eve said, "The gorge is two hundred miles long. Hiking to the right or left, along its rim is an issue because all the mountains on it are too steep to climb."

Mark said, "All our maps were wrong."

Gary asked, "Why did our RP screw up?"

RP, short for Route Planning software, creates topographic maps. I said, "Good question."

Venus drawled, "Another fuck up. Damn, my stomach hurts."

Eve said, "There is a forty percent chance that RP erred because airborne streptococcus interfered with its functionality."

Ben said, "It would have helped if we had noticed RP's

shortcomings earlier."

Dave sighed.

I said, "The only way to cross this is by using our SG."

If updrafts were strong enough, and you wanted to cross a canyon or gorge, you could push sleeved-mounted buttons. Within seconds SG, short for Suit Gliders, flaps popped out of the outer edges of our sleeves, hips, and pants and expanded. Then you jumped. At the same time, back-mounted jet motors, equipment that was the size of a human hair, switched on. As a result, one could ride air currents.

Dave glowered. "SG is tricky."

Gary looked down, a terrified expression on his face. "I agree. Too tricky."

Ben said, "Far too often, air currents shove you against a cliff and you die, crushed to death."

Jane hollered, "Don't remind me."

Eve said, "My quantum probability charts confirm that we must use the SG. It's the safest option."

Venus exclaimed, "It's a dumb-ass option."

Ben said, "Venus, you look exhausted."

"There is no fooling you."

"Venus, your sarcastic comment is useless."

"You better get used to it. That is the way I am."

I said, "SG's computers improve this tool every five hours."

Venus said, "I'll remember that just before I smash into a cliff."

A faint crunching grew louder. I turned and glanced in that direction.

In the near distance, a fifteen-foot long beast, a difficult to notice silhouette, partly hidden in shadows, crept toward me.

CHAPTER TWENTY-THREE

I pointed at it. "Can you see that predator?"
Venus said, "No. You're seeing something that isn't there."
Gary said, "The only things I see are several kapoks."
Mark said, "If it's there, I don't see it."
Jane added, "My DNAE can't detect it."
Eve said, "Mine does. Somehow, this predator has fooled your DNAE."
Jane asked, "Fooled it? How?"
Eve replied, "The entire crew should jump immediately. The beast will strike in eleven seconds."
Venus said, "Jumping scares me."
I suggested, "Do it or be torn to shreds."
Jane uttered, "I just noticed the beast's snout."
Venus said, "I don't. Wait. Now . . ."
Everybody turned, rushed toward the edge, and leaped.
As my adrenaline pumped faster, I dove, shot past a rock outcrop, flying through fine particles. At the same time, the headgear came out of my collar. Before long, a transparent mask covered my face. Harsh wind knocked the mask aside, about sixteenth of an inch. Would it rip the mask off?
I rose, a few feet, then dropped. Two thousand feet below me, in a river, white water surged. I glanced upward. About eight hundred feet away, a bird-like creature, barely noticeable because it was small, flew upward and landed on a tree, one of the hundreds, all on top of a cliff that was on the opposite side of the gorge.
I glanced to the right but didn't notice Eve or anybody else.

I looked to the left and spotted a triangular creature, an indigo species that was two hundred feet away, riding air currents, both wings fully extended.

I peered straight head. The cliff was sixty feet away. Before long I would crash into it.

CHAPTER TWENTY-FOUR

On my chest, tiny jet motors switched on. I rose, lowered both legs, landed on my feet, and stumbled. As my heart pounded harder, I crashed to the ground, between two bushes, about six feet beyond the cliff's edge.

In no time, I stood and hiked, searching for the others. Meanwhile, my face mask went inside my collar. In my contact lenses, warning text flashed, indicating that my DNAE was broken. The only way to find the others was by using the naked eye.

Not too long after, I asked, "Can anybody hear me?"

In the near distance, Gary announced, "Look up here."

I glanced in that direction.

About twenty feet away, thirty feet above the ground, he climbed down a lupuna.

I walked toward him. "Are you injured?"

"Just a few bruises."

I exhaled, trying to relax. "Is your DNAE intact?"

"Nope."

I shook my head, frustrated. "Let's search for everybody else."

"Sounds like a plan."

He shoved debris off his chin, and we trudged onward.

Before long Eve yelled, "Over here."

Gary said, "She is on the cliff."

Both of us marched in the direction, then looked down.

Sixty feet below us, she crawled over a two-inch-wide ledge.

I shuddered. "Can you make it?"

Gary said, "It's amazing that she hasn't fallen off. There is nothing to hold onto."

"Yes, amazing."

Her left foot slipped off a tiny ledge. Now she was dangling, holding onto a branch with her right hand.

Gary flinched. "She is in big trouble."

My guts tightened in shocked response. To reach this spot, she had to climb sixty feet straight up a smooth rock face.

Her left hand changed into a drill. Much to my surprise, its tip bored a hole in the cliff. A tether with a spike at its top end shot out of her right sleeve. Within seconds, the spike landed in a crack that was forty feet above her. The drill's tip came out of the hole. Presently, she rose, pulled upward by the tether. When she was forty feet higher, our colleague placed both feet on a narrow ledge.

Gary said, "Astounding."

Eve jumped, and landed on our right, between two small bushes.

I blurted, "That was surprising."

She nodded. "Did you see Dave?"

"No."

"He crashed into the cliff."

Gary cringed. "Where?"

Eve said, "Eighty feet below me."

I asked, "Is he okay?"

Eve's silver cornea turned to gold. "To the contrary. After the crash, he fell eight hundred feet and died."

I recoiled.

Gary said, "What a horrible way to go."

"A valid comment."

I asked, "Eve, why did your cornea change colors?"

"It was organizing photos of Dave's corpse."

My teeth chattered in a nervous response. "Eve, my DNAE is broken, wrecked by my rough landing. Can yours spot the rest of the crew?"

"To the contrary. On the plus side, it is attempting to repair itself."

Gary said, "More trouble."

I said, "Let's spread out."

Everybody did.

Within the hour, we located the others. All of them had touched down on different trees and climbed down.

Mark said, "Tom, I want to go my own way because of your poor leadership."

I cringed, upset by his decision. "Okay."

Mark asked, "Who wants to accompany me?"

Jane said, "Me."

Venus said, "Count me in. Tom is a poor planner."

My stomach muscles tightened in frustration.

Ben raised his hand. "Following Mark is a good idea."

Gary nodded. "Venus' point is a great idea."

I sighed, disappointed. "Eve?"

"Tom, I'll accompany you."

I blinked, surprised. "Eve and I can't keep in touch with each other or the rest of you because our lenses' TTO can't repair itself."

Mark frowned. "That is too bad. Oh well."

I said, "Ben, export the plant species, the ones on the plateau, into my lenses."

"Why should I?"

"If Eve and I don't see you again, finding those plants will be tough, if not impossible."

Ben scowled. "Don't worry about it. See you on the plateau."

Eve said, "Ben, Tom's statement is correct. Exporting that database into his lenses or mine is a good decision."

"Don't worry about it. See you on the plateau."

I asked, "Ben, what are the names of those plants?"

"Because they're a new species, I made up names for them, Runus and Zama."

The rest of the crew departed.

I said, "Splitting up is a bad idea. Now, it's easier for a Balor or another predator to kill them because there are only five in their group."

"A true statement. Mark and the others should have analyzed their situation more carefully as opposed to making a decision based on irrational disappointment."

I sighed. "And there are only two of us. It will be easier for a Balor or something to kill us."

"That is a valid comment."

My mind kicked into overdrive, an attempt to figure out how to deal with the next attack. "Let's go."

"As you wish."

My colleague and I tramped on.

After passing sabal palmettos, we came upon thick underbrush. Ahead, some of it crumbled, creating a narrow path.

I blinked, surprised. "Why did it fall apart?"

"Twenty minutes ago, my bio-logic board's software created SFDT, short for Strong Force Disabling Tool. As a result, these plants fell apart."

"Amazing." The strong force, part of every plant or animal's subatomic structure, kept these life forms intact.

Eve nodded.

"What is that odd smell?"

"A Hunig is on our right, hiding behind fucus."

My adrenaline pumped faster. "Let's keep going."

"A wise decision."

Two hours later, laser beams came out of Eve's wrist and killed thousands of ants. "These insects are filled with protein."

I recoiled, grabbed some, shoved them in my mouth, and chewed. "They taste awful."

"Nonetheless, they are a necessary meal."

Our waist-mounted pouches opened.

Eve's hands changed into large spoons. She scooped up the ants and dumped them into our pouches. The pouches closed immediately, and we trekked.

At dusk, after crossing four streams, all dimly lit, filled with pink two-inch worms, repulsive invertebrates, we halted in a small open space. I said, "Let's camp here."

"I'll stand guard the entire night."

"Thanks."

Not long after dawn, both of us departed.

I yawned. "This heat is wearing me out."

"Has your suit's air conditioner malfunctioned?"

"It did that a day after we crash-landed."

"At this point, the heat hasn't affected my bio-logic boards or nano engines. I just exported ACR into your suit's air conditioner. There is a twenty percent chance that ACR can service your air conditioner."

"Hopefully it can." ACR, short for Air Conditioner Repair, was unpredictable.

We pushed aside branches. A dark silhouette, about seven-feet tall, barely noticeable in the gloom, rushed toward us.

I quivered.

The beast squealed. *Eeeeeom.* Suddenly it veered to the left.

I asked, "Where did it go?"

"It is sixty feet away from this spot, moving toward another location."

"Why did it take off?"

"My SFDT destroyed some of its teeth. As a result, it fled."

"That is a handy weapon."

"A valid comment." My colleague and I resumed the journey.

In the late afternoon, we reached the bottom of a cliff. At the top of this four-thousand-foot-high obstacle, winged creatures flew toward kapoks, trees that were on the edge of the plateau. I sighed. "Climbing this will be tiresome."

She nodded.

I stepped on a ledge, then hiked upward.

Before long, we passed holes, ones that were inside a steep cliff.

Inside them, something brayed. *Hooonk.*

I cringed. "What made that noise? My DNAE can't ID the creature."

"A nine-foot-long worm."

"Is it dangerous?"

"Its teeth are two inches long. My DNAE repaired itself several minutes ago. Now it is searching through databases. Although this invertebrate is similar to a Lono worm, a species found in Jata, a jungle in the United Provinces, this worm's teeth might be used to chew roots, not attack us or any other fauna."

I ground my teeth together, disappointed by this vague answer.

Without warning, the worm jerked its head upward. Much to my surprise, its lower jaw crumbled, and its head dropped to the ground.

I asked, "Did you kill it?"

"I did. Although it is an ugly species, its body is filled with protein."

"Ugly is right." I yanked the creature out of the hole and shoved it into my waist-mounted pouch.

Both of us reached the top of the cliff, then hiked into the jungle.

I said, "My DNAE's evaluation screen is filled meaningless equations, a sign that this tool is broken."

"All the equations on mine are useless. Quantum computer model F has determined that my DNAE's utility function can repair my DNAE in thirty minutes."

I bit my lip, frustrated. "It would help if we could find Ben."

"Indeed."

"Can you use SP to locate the Runus and Zama?"

"Its screen is blank. It is broken."

I shook my head, frustrated.

"If Ben had exported Runus and Zama descriptions into the other's lenses and we found our colleagues, locating those species will be easier."

"Yes."

Without warning, a dark creature rushed out of the shadows, then slashed Eve's neck.

CHAPTER TWENTY-FIVE

Her head dropped behind her.
As my adrenaline pumped harder, the predator, a quick-moving blur, clawed my right arm. Without warning, it screeched. *Vooot*. Much to my surprise, it, a barely noticeable silhouette, mostly hidden in the gloom, sprinted away and vanished into the jungle.

"Eve, are you alive?"

She turned, revealing her head, a body part that was upside down, eight inches below the back of her neck, held in place by several cables. "A valid question."

I recoiled. "You look terrible."

"Correct."

"Can you repair yourself?"

"There is a thirty percent chance I can. However, accomplishing this goal will take anywhere from two to nine hours."

"Can you see where you are going?"

"It will be a difficult process. Your assistance would make the task easier."

"Did you get a good look at the predator that attacked us?"

"No." The cables hummed.

"I didn't either. It moved too fast."

"Why are your cables making that noise?"

"It is part of the repair process."

I blinked, nervous.

Faraway, somewhere to our left, hidden behind foliage, something squawked. *Kooka*.

I flinched. "My DNAE can't ID that creature. Let's search

for the others. In the meantime, your DNAE might repair itself. If that happens, finding Runus and the other plant will be easier." We marched. Nanites began suturing my wound. At the same time, they injected T cells into it. As a result, the injury would heal faster.

Within the hour we came upon Mark, Ben, and Venus.

Venus scowled. "What happened to Eve? She looks terrible."

Eve replied., "A poorly lit predator attacked me."

Mark trembled.

Ben gasped, "Wow."

Mark said, "Tom, you're injured."

I mentioned the attack.

Mark flinched.

Venus called out, "What a mess."

I asked, "Where is everybody else?"

Mark said, "Two days ago, in the late afternoon, before we scaled the cliff that led to the plateau, Gary and Jane left, searching for food. They never returned."

Eve asked, "Did you look for them?"

Venus snapped, "Of course. What a stupid question."

I asked, "Did you search for a few hours, an entire day, or what?"

Mark said, "An entire day."

Eve asked, "You didn't find any trace of them?"

Venus said, "Quit complaining. We did the best we could."

Eve said, "I'm not complaining. I just want to know more about your effort."

Venus frowned.

Mark, a distraught expression on his face, sighed.

Ben said, "I found several Runus and Zama nearby."

I said, "Let's take a look at them." Everybody departed.

After hiking between towering ferns, dimly lit flora in a gloomy part of the jungle, our group came upon a six-foot high bush, a species with orange and crimson leaves.

Eve asked, "Is this a Runus?"

Ben said, "You bet."

I asked, "Have you tried to convert it into an engine?"

Ben glowered. "Yes. I made three attempts."

Eve asked, "What happened?"

Venus snapped, "Nothing. Ben's project is a fucking failure. We've come all this way for nothing."

Mark sighed. "Unfortunately, Venus is correct."

I asked, "Where is a Zama?"

Ben said, "It's a short walk from here."

Venus asked, "Why bother?"

Eve said, "Venus, you sound disappointed."

"I sure am. Ben tried six times and the plant didn't change."

My jaw muscles tightened. "I want to see this plant."

Venus said, "Going there is a waste of time."

I said, "Let me be the judge of that."

Venus glared at me.

Ben said, "Venus, you give up too easily."

"I'm a realist. You should listen to me."

Mark said, "Venus is pragmatic."

I said, "Let's go."

Venus said, "Tom, you're a stubborn dreamer, don't care about facts."

"Maybe. However, I want to see the Zama. Going there won't hurt."

Mark shrugged. The entire group trekked.

Within minutes everybody passed animal scat.

I cringed, then pointed at them. "Are those Notak droppings?"

Eve said, "They are."

Venus said, "I hate this spot. It's darker than the surrounding area. The mist makes it hard to see most of the plants. There is a lot of alien mold on just about every leaf. This location reminds me of places from prehistoric times, long before humans, Aito, or any other race existed."

Mark said, "Venus' statement rings true. I don't want to stay in this area for too long."

I said, "Mark, you've spent a long time in the jungle."

"Yes, but this area is different."

Eve asked, "How is it different?"

Mark said, "The alien mold is filled with lethal viruses. Brushing against the mold could be dangerous."

I quivered. "Understood."

Before long the entire group reached a nine-foot-tall bush, a species with thousands of tiny ochre leaves. Between the leaves, dew fell off gray berries.

Ben pointed at the plant. "This is a Zama."

Venus said, "It isn't much to look at."

Mark said, "I agree with Venus."

Ben remarked, "My DNAE just exported exons into the Zama's leaves."

Exons were part of an organism's genome.

Venus blurted, "Nothing is happening. Another failure."

Much to my surprise, the plant started growing.

Eve said, "Amazing."

Chapter Twenty-six

M ark said, "This didn't happen before."
Venus blurted, "It's . . ."
Ben said, "My newly created exons are changing the plant."
Eve said, "An interesting transformation."

Within minutes, the plant was thirty feet high, ten feet in diameter, covered by green layers, like corn. To its left, seven Zamas, much small than this one, started growing.

Presently all seven were the same height as the thirty-foot high one. Without warning, the coverings on all eight opened.
Mark asked, "Why did they open?"
Eve said, "Based on three quantum computer models, if you step inside the Zama, the coverings close, sealing you inside. Then the plant shoots you into space, like a seed."
Venus announced, "I don't believe it. Plants don't shoot humans, Aito, or any other humanoids into space."
Eve said, "All three computer models provided accurate information."
Mark asked, "How do you know they're accurate?"
Eve said, "They're based on quantum modeling, use the most energy effect mode to achieve a goal."
Mark scowled. "Yes, supposedly like protein folding."
Eve said, "A valid assertion."
Venus glowered. "Why hasn't anybody created this kind of plant before?"

Ben said, "Because the Zama is unique."

Venus sighed.

Mark shook his head.

Venus said, "I'm not going to step inside these plants."

I asked, "Why not?"

Venus said, "The walls are too thin, will fall apart when the Zama reaches Heja's outer atmosphere."

Eve said, "My computer model . . ."

Venus snapped, "I don't care about the computer model."

Mark said, "Don't cut off Eve before she finishes her statement."

Venus said, "Her statement is based on a fantasy, isn't worth listening to."

I said, "Venus, you have to be more flexible."

She said, "You have to be more realistic."

My jaw muscles tightened.

Mark asked, "Will there be enough oxygen inside the Zama to sustain us?"

Eve said, "My computer model has confirmed that there is."

Venus said, "Your computer model is wrong, uses fake assumptions."

I said, "Climbing into the Zama and going into space is the best plan. If we stay here, a predator will eventually kill us."

Mark, a doubtful expression on his face, scratched his jaw.

Venus, an angry look on her face, squinted.

Ben, a gloomy expression his face, wiped the sweat off his chin.

I said, "Venus, you aren't saying anything."

She clenched her teeth.

Mark blinked. "This is a tough decision."

Before long, a distant crunching, barely audible, grew louder.

Eve said, "A Notak is on our right, coming closer."

Venus glowered. "I can't see or hear it."

My adrenaline started pumping. I pointed in that direction. "Its claw is between those leaves."

Mark blurted, "I see it. It's moving to the left, waiting for the best moment to strike."

Ben exclaimed, "Appalling."

I said, "It's time to climb inside a Zama."

Venus frowned. "Are you kidding?"

I said, "Staying here is too dangerous."

Venus paused, a grim expression on her face. "The beast might leave."

I said, "If it attacks, somebody will be injured or die."

Mark spat, "Damn."

I said, "Each Zama is only big enough for one person."

Ben said, "Obviously."

I rushed toward the plant, jumped inside and its walls snapped shut. Without warning, it lurched upward.

CHAPTER TWENTY-SEVEN

I asked, "Can anybody hear me?"
Outside, beyond the opaque walls, gusting wind became louder.

I clenched my teeth. A helmet, equipment with a face mask, came out of my collar and covered my head.

In my lenses, the time pointed out that four minutes had passed since I entered the Zama.

Two hours later, the Zama jerked forward. At the same time, its walls lurched downward, revealing a small room.

On the opposite wall, a door vanished. An Aito humanoid with blue skin, a stranger who was dressed in an Afan Space Command uniform, entered. "Who are you?"

I answered.

"My name is Captain Olar. You're lucky we found you. The plant you're in was orbiting Heja."

I blinked, surprised. "Were you searching for us?"

"No, we were fleeing several of Veen's galactic battle cruisers."

"Who is Veen?"

"A dictator who conquered Afan."

I quivered. "All of it?"

He frowned. "I'm not sure. Three of my crew, including me, jumped inside this ship, named the Camor, and left."

My mind sped up, trying to accept this shocking news. "Will you return to Afan?"

"Not for a while. We'll have to land on Heja and hide in one of its jungles. If we're lucky, Veen's galactic battle cruisers or interstellar war craft won't spot the Camor. Quite often they use laser probes to detect freedom fighter ships like this. If they don't notice it, they leave."

I told him about the Notak and other beasts.

"We have weapons, can fight those predators."

"But it's dangerous."

He glowered. "They don't have laser cannons, MOS and other types of guns. We do."

I exhaled, trying to calm down. MOS, short for Molecular Scramblers, broke apart chemical compounds. As a result, some parts of a humanoid, human, or a beast disintegrated, and they died. "Have you picked up other members of my crew?"

"Not yet. Let's go to the bridge." Both of us walked toward the wall. Most of it disappeared, but we kept going.

On our left, an Aito woman with turquoise skin, a stranger who was in a floating chair, facing a gigantic three-D holographic replica of Heja, asked, "Captain, who is he?"

He answered. Then he pointed at her. "Tom, this is crew member Rova."

A Qio with striped skin, a man in another floating chair, said, "Tom, welcome aboard. My name is Inom."

I smiled.

The captain said, "Tom, have a seat." He pointed at a floating chair. I sat. My lenses sent neutrinos into Captain Boris Olar's mind. They returned.

He was born in Govo, a town in Keec. When he was nine, he bought a three-D holographic game called Makto. Although his mother complained, saying it was a waste of money, he played Makto every day because he loved shooting at gigantic snakes.

He received a bachelor's of Science and a master's,

majoring in Flightpath Vectors. Two weeks after graduating, Eval Airways hired him.

My lenses sent neutrinos into Rova's mind. Alice Rova received her bachelor's and master's in Science, majoring in Flight Path Algorithms. For the last two years, she helped fly B-thirty-threes, commercial spacecraft that traveled between Afan and Ejj. This information vanished.

My lenses sent neutrinos into Inom's mind. He received his bachelor's and master's in science, majoring in Aeronautics.

Two weeks after receiving his diploma, Nolan Airways hired him.

Fifteen minutes later, Inom pointed at a yellow screen. "A Zama is between space debris, rocks. Hopefully, one of your colleagues is inside the plant."

I shuddered. "I hope so, too."

To his left Rova frowned. "We have to be careful. If our ship crashes into the rocks, air will leak out of the hull and everybody aboard will die."

Chills raced down my back.

The Camor veered to starboard and halted close to a rock, bumping against the hull.

Olar asked, "Any damage?"

Inom commented, "Just a minor scratch."

Captain Olar sighed. "We were lucky."

Rova said, "Correct."

On a blue screen, Camor's port side hatch opened. The Zama lurched inside this craft, pulled in by a gravitational tool. Within seconds the hatch closed.

I left the bridge, then walked inside another room. Without warning, the Zama opened. Eve stepped out of it. Her head was still behind her neck.

I blinked, surprised. "Eve, are you okay?"

"I am intact, no skin lacerations or trauma. All my nanites, lenses, internal software, optic and auditory systems, along with my bio-logic boards are operating at one hundred percent."

I exhaled, releasing the tension, and repeated Captain Olar's decision.

"Has he considered all the options?"

"Yes."

"Returning there is dangerous."

I nodded, my teeth clenched. "When will your head return to its original position?"

"Three statistical tables, all based on backpropagating neural network problem solving, estimate that it could be anywhere from one week to a month."

I sighed. Like the human brain, backpropagating neural networks learned by their mistakes and improved.

Within the hour we picked up the others. I told them about our current status.

Venus howled, "Going back to Heja is a fucking stupid idea."

I blinked.

Mark cringed.

Ben examined his trembling hand. "Oh my god." Everybody left the room and entered the bridge.

On screen, an arrow-shaped intergalactic ship appeared.

Inom announced, "Captain, that is the Loto, one of Veen's interstellar battlecruisers."

"How far away is it?"

"Eight hundred miles."

Inom announced, "It just fired at us."

A laser blast struck the Camor's portside.

Inom announced, "Captain, that direct hit destroyed a communication satellite dish."

Captain Olar said, "Land at coordinates twelve-four-zero."

I shook. "That's in the spot we just left."

Venus shouted, "Going there is nuts."

A laser blast whizzed by the starboard side.

Chapter Twenty-eight

The Camor dropped, then raced toward the moon's surface.

Captain Olar asked, "Rova, Inom, is the Loto following us?"

Rova said, "It is."

Within fifteen minutes, the Camor touched down between towering kapoks.

Rova said, "The Loto is five miles above the plateau, probing its surface with SRE."

SRE, Shape Recognition Software, measured forms and compared them with archives.

Captain Olar remarked, "Switch on ASO."

ASO, short for Alternative Surface Organizer, created facades. Onscreen text pointed out that one second ago, because of ASO the Camor changed. Now the ship resembled a lupuna.

Eve asked, "Captain Olar, does the Loto have SDA?"

SDA, a short term for Surface Detector Analyzer, probed thousands of objects per second, looking for cloaked space ships.

"Undetermined."

I asked, "Captain Olar, why aren't there more crew aboard the Camor?"

"There wasn't enough time to pick up more. One of Veen's armies, a battle group consisting of tanks, BRR, and infantry, invaded our spaceport. All three of us jumped inside this craft and took off."

BRR was short for Battle Ready Robots. I asked, "Captain, is there any food aboard your ship?"

He grimaced. "No."

Venus glowered. "Why not?"

Rova scowled. "There wasn't time to gather any."

I said, "It's time to gather legumes, berries, and mushrooms. I need volunteers."

Rova said, "I'll go with you."

Inom said, "Count me in."

Venus said, "Rova and Inom, both of you are crazy to do this."

Rova said, "My MDE is a great weapon."

MDE was short for Molecular Destabilizer. I said, "Great, let's go."

Eve said, "I would go but until my head is back on top of my body, seeing any beasts clearly enough so that I shoot and hit them would be difficult."

Mark sighed.

Venus said, "Eve, you're useless. My guess is that you won't ever return to normal."

Eve kept staring at the sky.

Mark said, "Venus, you're too pessimistic."

All three of us departed.

Rova said, "Tom, my contact lenses can't send you any text messages, three-D holograms, or emails. For some unrevealed cause, they've stopped working."

I recoiled.

Inom said, "I'm having the same difficulty."

Rova asked, "Tom, why is this happening?"

"My crew and I had this problem. My best guess is that airborne bacteria, an alien organism that isn't on my database is causing this."

Rova hesitated, a dour expression on her face.

Inom snapped, "Damn it. It's impossible to contact Captain Olar or anybody else."

Before long we entered a dimly lit spot, an area surrounded by towering bushes. An eight-foot-tall creature, barely notice-able in the dark mist, rushed toward us.

CHAPTER TWENTY-NINE

It slashed Inom's shoulder. He screamed, "Hel . . ."
Bullets struck the predator. It screeched. *Eeeeeen*. In one quick motion, it veered to the right and darted into thick mist.

I asked, "Can anybody see the creature?"

Rova said, "No, it's hiding in the fog."

Inom added, "My neck hurts like hell."

I said, "It's bleeding nonstop." I sprayed the injury with Genetic Designed Solution, medicine that was created for Inom's DNA. As a result, his white blood cells and antigens would attack any bacteria and the wound could heal faster. Within seconds, the bleeding stopped.

Rova said, "The beast is on our right, fifteen feet away."

I called out, "I don't see it."

She pointed in that direction.

It rushed out from behind a bush.

Both of us fired at it. It howled. *Oooooot*. Without warning, it dropped to the ground, mucus pouring out of its chest.

I squeezed the trigger. A laser beam from my gun tore the creature's body in half.

To our left, a faint scratching grew louder.

Rova called out, "Another predator is nearby."

I looked up, then glanced in that direction. "It's hiding in the mist."

Rova said, "Precisely. After I spotted its claw, the only part of it that was visible, it retreated into the haze."

Inom said, "Let's go back to the Camor. This area is too dangerous."

I said, "We must locate our next meal. My last DNAE probe has determined that the only accessible legumes and berries in this area are on our right, a short walk from this spot. The rest are at the top of tough-to-climb steep cliffs."

Rova glared at me.

Inom glowered. "Tom, searching for our next meal is a lousy idea."

Rova said, "Tom is correct."

Inom said, "I'll go ahead with the plan, but if that beast kills us, remember that I warned you."

I said, "Understood."

Our small group hiked. Without warning, it started raining. Much to my surprise, it turned into a downpour.

Inom said, "It's impossible to see anything clearly."

Rova said, "No doubt about it."

A seven-foot-tall creature, just a barely noticeable silhouette, dashed toward our group.

I pointed at it. "Look . . ."

Rova cried out, "What the . . ."

While chills ran up my spine, I fired at the silhouette.

It screeched. *Ooooolooo.*

Inom spun around and stumbled.

Oooolooo. The beast raced around everybody, then stopped a few feet beyond Rova.

Her knuckle-mounted weapon, two inches long, chattered. *Kek, kek, kek.*

Olllllooo. It sprinted into the jungle.

I said, "Rova, good shot."

Inom slowly rose to his feet. "I broke my arm."

I said, "It will take ISO several weeks to repair it." ISO, short for Injury Solution application, injected nanites and chemicals into the injury. The chemicals enhanced any patient's antibodies along with their white blood cells.

Inom groaned. "It hurts."

I said, "Let's gather food, then return to Camor."

Rova glared at me. "If you say so. However, I don't like it."
Our small group trekked.

In a short while, we came upon thorn trees. I said, "These are edible."

Inom glared at me. "Are you sure?"

"Yes."

Everybody grabbed one and yanked it out. Our belt-mounted pouches opened. We tore off the roots, ones with bulging legumes on them, then shoved them into our pouches.

About twenty feet away, hidden in the mist, a rustling grew louder.

Inom blurted, "A beast is watching us."

Rova exclaimed, "It will strike any moment."

I said, "Hold your fire. After we gather more legumes, let's go."

Inom asked, "Hold our fire?"

I said, "Correct."

Rova blurted, "Holding our fire is a bad idea."

About eight feet away, the beast stuck its snout out of swirling mist. I pointed at it. "Can you see it?"

Rova shoved more legumes into her pouch. "Not yet."

Inom blurted, "Look at its teeth. That thing could tear us to pieces."

CHAPTER THIRTY

Rova looked up. "It's hideous."
I fired at the predator.

Olllllo. Its snout retreated into the fog.

I said, "We might have scared it off. Let's go."

Everybody turned, then slogged onward.

Rova asked, "Why isn't that creature on my DNAE's screen?"

Inom said, "An important question. It isn't on mine either."

I said, "Airborne viruses could have crippled our DNAE."

Inom bellowed, "Chaos."

Rova said, "Ugly chaos."

Our group continued on.

At dusk, we reached the Camor.

Captain Olar asked, "Did you have any difficulties?"

Rova answered.

Venus said, "You should have been more careful."

Rova said, "We did the best we could."

Mark scowled.

At dawn, Inom, Rova, Venus and I stepped out of the Camor.

I yawned.

Venus said, "Those legumes taste like shit."

Inom said, "You complain too much."

Venus burst out, "So do you."

Inom said, "You're talking nonsense."

"Shut up. You talk too much."

"You're rude."

"I tell it like it is. Get used to it."

About sixteen feet away, three Notak jumped out from behind ferns.

Inom pointed at them. "Look out."

My adrenaline pumped harder.

CHAPTER THIRTY-ONE

Venus snapped, "They're—"
I said, "Fire at will."
Venus tripped.
The shortest Notak's chest exploded.
The tallest Notak lunged at me.
I dodged to the left.
The skinniest beast veered to the right.
A particle beam struck the tallest Notak. It bellowed. *Aaaatay.* Much to my surprise, it spun around and dashed into the jungle.
The skinniest rushed toward Venus.
Bullets struck its jaw. *Aaaaatay.* It slashed Venus' shoulder.
She screamed.
A laser beam hit its neck. *Aaaatay.* It spun around, then sprinted away.
I stooped.
As blood gushed out of Venus' wounds, she bellowed, "I'm bleeding to death."
Eve arrived, then sprayed medication onto the injury.
I said, "The bleeding has stopped."
Venus said, "Tom, you're experienced, should have been watching out for us."
Inom said, "Venus, Tom, and the rest of us drove them off."
Rova said, "Inom is correct. Those predators were fast. Tom did a great job."
I asked, "Who fired that laser?"
Rova said, "That was me."

I said, "You're handy."

"Thanks."

Rova asked, "Who fired that particle beam?"

Inom said, "I did."

Rova said, "Your aim was great."

Inom offered a quick smile.

Venus said, "If all of you were better, you would have killed those beasts before they attacked me."

Inom frowned. "You're alive. They could have killed you."

Venus glared at him.

Captain Olar arrived. "Venus, you're injured. What happened?

I answered, "Three Notak attacked us."

Captain Olar said, "These are the most aggressive beasts I've ever seen."

Eve said, "Quantum probability charts confirmed that there was a twenty percent chance they would strike six hours after the Camor touched down."

Captain Olar said, "Too many robots are flawed. Your charts are pointless."

I said, "TAS is well designed."

Captain Olar said, "Tom, every FSR was flawed."

FSR, short for Field Support Robots, was created nineteen years before the first TAS. I said, "That is correct. However, TAS is better."

Inom looked at me, an irritated expression on his face. "I agree with Captain Olar."

My stomach muscles tightened.

Rova said, "I agree with Captain Olar and Inom."

Venus glowered.

Mark arrived. "What happened to Venus?"

Inom replied.

Mark asked, "Did anybody pay attention to Eve's predictions regarding the Notak?"

Rova answered.

Mark scowled. "It's too bad that you don't trust Eve. She is a big help."

Captain Olar gave Mark a dirty look. "I'll be the judge of that."

Two hours later, two bullet-shaped craft, both eighty feet long, arrived and stopped eighty feet above the Camor.

Rova pointed at them. "Those are RC, part of Veen's intergalactic force."

I grimaced. RC was short for Reconnaissance Craft. Helmets came out of everybody's shoulder pads and covered our heads.

Both RC fired laser beams at the Camor.

CHAPTER THIRTY-TWO

Rova, Inom, Captain Olar, and I blasted the intruders. Inom blurted, "My last shot hit one ship's nose."

Captain Olar exclaimed, "Mine struck the other ship's starboard side."

Without warning, both RC took off.

Rova asked, "Where did they go?"

Captain Olar said, "My IHD has just revealed they landed ninety feet from here, hidden behind kapoks."

IHD was short for a tiny wrist-mounted Infrared Heat Detector. My adrenaline pumped harder.

Eve, Mark, and Venus stepped out of Camor.

Eve said, "Sorry we are late. We were eating."

Rova said, "Eve, your head is on top of your neck."

I blinked, surprised.

Eve nodded.

I asked, "Eve, can you help us search for the RC's crew?"

"A valid request."

Captain Olar asked, "Can Eve help us, and not break down?"

I said, "No doubt about it. She can."

Rova said, "Every FSR was flawed."

Mark said, "Eve is a TAS."

Rova frowned. "I've heard about TAS, don't know much about them."

Mark said, "Trust me, Eve is a great soldier."

Rova clenched her teeth.

Captain Olar's forehead tightened. "Somebody needs to

hike through the jungle, find out how many enemy soldiers we have to fight. Who will volunteer for this mission?"

I raised my hand.

Olar asked, "Anybody else?"

Eve said, "Me."

Venus said, "Count me in."

I blinked, surprised. "Let's go."

All three of us departed.

I said, "Let's communicate by hand signals. That way enemy soldiers are less likely to notice us."

Venus scowled.

Eve nodded.

Within minutes, our crew entered a gloomy place where mist partly obscured dew-covered ferns and other plants.

In a jiffy, we hiked between towering strangler figs. Eve crouched. At the same time, she created a zero with her forefingers and thumb, indicating that she hadn't noticed any of the RC's crew.

Venus copied Eve's hand signal.

A laser blast grazed my left knee.

CHAPTER THIRTY-THREE

I dove to the ground, then pointed upward, indicating that the enemy, a sniper, was somewhere above us.

Venus fired. *Kek, kek, kek.*

Bullets came out of my shoulder-mounted rifle, a one-inch long weapon. Forty-feet away, an Aito woman soldier, dressed in a camouflaged suit, fell off a branch and crashed to the ground.

Venus raised her fist, a triumphant gesture.

I rose to my feet, then all three of us advanced slowly.

Four enemy soldiers rushed out from behind a wall of vines, their arm-mounted pistols blazing. *Nik, Nik, Nik.*

All three of us dove to the ground.

My weapon jammed. *Oot, oot, oot.*

Venus shrieked, "I'm hit."

Eve's firearm went off. *Yeeep, yeep.*

All four soldiers collapsed. One moaned and went silent.

I glanced to the right.

A laser blast had struck the top of Venus' left arm, half an inch below her shoulder. Although nanites in her suit had stopped the bleeding, her arm was dangling, held in place by several muscles.

Eve said, "Venus, this arm will have to be replaced by a robotic body part."

Venus shook. "Can't you save my arm?"

Eve said, "That is impossible."

Venus sucked in air through clenched teeth.

Eve said, "Although SN will inject morphine into the

injury, the next step will hurt somewhat."

Venus started crying. "Do it."

SN was short for Surgical Nanites.

CHAPTER THIRTY-FOUR

Eve said, "You will feel a pinch." SN flew out of her collar and sliced off Venus' arm.

She blurted, "Owww."

ORN, short for Organized Nano robots, came out of Eve's wrist and slowly created an android arm, one that was chrome colored.

Venus raised it, then flexed her fingers. "It feels odd, but it works."

I blinked, surprised that the artificial limb functioned properly on the first try.

In no time, the chrome body part turned orange, matching the rest of Venus' body.

I said, "Let's go." Our small group trekked.

Within thirty minutes, we stopped behind seven-foot-high undergrowth, then peeked between its leaves. Thirty feet away, twenty-five enemy soldiers marched out of an RC.

I whispered into Eve's ear, "There are too many of them. Let's go back to the Camor and tell the others what we have found. Share this conversation with Venus."

She murmured into Venus' ear. Our small group departed.

We reached the ship. I asked, "Where is Captain Olar?"

Ben glowered. "Twenty minutes ago, a Balor rushed out of the shadows, bit his head off, then dragged that along with his body into the jungle."

Venus' eyes opened wider. "Oh my god. Why didn't you

kill the beast?"

Ben scowled. "Mark and Captain Olar were outside the Camor. Everybody else was inside."

Venus glared at him. "That is no excuse."

Ben spat, "Let me finish."

Venus sighed.

"It's dark, hard to see clearly. Mark told me that both of them fired at the creature and might have grazed it. In less than a second, the predator dashed off, taking the Captain with it."

Mark stepped out of the Camor. "I heard that. Ben's description is accurate."

As my mind raced, trying to figure out what we could do to avoid tragic scenarios like this, I said, "Understood."

Eve nodded.

Everybody else came out of the ship.

Rova said, "I think Tom should take over."

Inom said, "Great idea. Whoever agrees, raise their hand."

Everybody but Venus did.

Eve asked, "Venus, why do you disagree?"

She crossed both arms over her chest. "I have mixed feelings about it."

I said, "Okay. Everybody should hike toward the enemy ships. When we arrive, spread out and kill as many as possible, before they detect our positions. Then retreat a.s.a.p."

Venus said, "I hate it."

I asked, "Do you have a better plan?"

She shook her head.

Our band all spread out, halting behind undergrowth.

I glanced between leaves. Thirty feet away, twenty enemy soldiers, all seated, laughed. One, a Qio woman with orange skin, grabbed a wafer and shoved it in her mouth.

Two Notak rushed out of the shadows and attacked two

soldiers.

One screamed.

CHAPTER THIRTY-FIVE

Most of them scattered. Two dodged to the right. Three fired their weapons. The beasts ducked, then raced, sliced off arms, and bit off heads.

Before long all the soldier's bodies spread out.

I whispered in Eve's ear, "The predators moved so fast that fighting them off will be tough." I raised my hand, then spread my fingers apart, indicating that our band should retreat before the Notak and other soldiers noticed us.

When our group reached a halfway point between the attack and the Camor, I asked, "Can anybody think of a technique we can use to defeat the enemy soldiers and the Notak?"

Inom sighed.

Ben glowered.

Rova paused, her brow tight.

Ahead, Venus glanced over her shoulder. "Absolutely not. All of us are going to die."

Eve said, "An intriguing question."

Mark said, "If I export genetic code into sabal palmetto that is close to the enemy ships, the trees might shoot seeds. The seeds could scare the soldiers. As a result, they would fire at them. After realizing they are harmless, the soldiers would stop shooting. At that point, because they are weary, our group should attack the enemy soldiers."

Venus said, "It's a bad idea."

Mark glared at her. "Do you have a better one?"

Venus said, "Don't give me a hard time."

Ben said, "We're out of options. Mark's plan is better than nothing."

Eve said, "My quantum probability table has determined there is a thirty percent chance that his plan will succeed."

I blinked, frustrated by her comment. "Eve, let's forget about that table."

She stared at me, a vacant expression in her eyes.

Inom looked down his nose at me.

Rova coughed, a worried expression on her face.

I said, "Okay, let's do it." Our entire group turned, then hiked toward the enemy ships.

We reached a group of sabal palmetto.

Mark said, "I just exported the genetic code."

Venus whispered, "The trees aren't doing anything. What a stupid idea."

Inom sighed.

Rova bit her lip.

Ben clenched his teeth.

I blenched, disappointed.

Much to my surprise, the trees sprayed seeds.

Enemy soldiers rushed out of their spacecraft, blasting.

Chapter Thirty-six

Eve murmured in my ear, "Success."
I nodded.

Within minutes, the enemy troops stopped shooting.

Our group discharged our weapons.

Caught off guard, our foes discharged their weapons aimlessly.

All of them were now dead.

Eve said, "Mark's plan succeeded."

Venus said, "It was pure luck."

Mark glared at her. "It was a well-thought-out plan."

Venus gave him a cocky look.

Inom said, "Although I was skeptical, the results are impressive."

Rova said, "*Very* impressive."

I said, "Let's go back to the Camor. It's time to leave Heja."

Our entire group slogged on.

Minutes later, we passed between towering fucus, trees that blocked out most of the sky. Somewhere in the darkness, a creature hooted. *Ooma, Ooma.*

I shuddered. "What made that noise?"

Mark said, "Airborne huicungo seeds spreading out in three directions confirms that a Notak did. The creature is telling another member of its species that it enjoys hunting and eating its prey."

Eve said, "A fascinating observation."

Venus said, "Seeds can't translate these predators' sounds."

Mark asked, "Are you questioning my judgment?"

Venus said, "Somebody has to. Your comment regarding the seed's translation is a fantasy."

My stomach muscles tightened. Was Venus' cynicism accurate? I couldn't tell. "Let's pay attention to our surroundings. If Mark is correct, we're in big trouble."

Ben quivered, then glanced in several directions, his arm raised, ready to fire.

Inom examined his trembling hand and stuck out his arm. "I'm ready."

Rova clenched her teeth.

Our band marched on.

We came upon the Camor, its port side smashed.

CHAPTER THIRTY-SEVEN

Eve said, "My scan indicates the laser blasts that demolished the Camor came from a destroyer, part of Veen's fleet."

Mark scowled. "I wasn't expecting this."

Venus said, "Tom, you should have ordered Inom or somebody else to stay here and protect our ship."

"If you or somebody else remained here, you would be dead."

Venus snapped, "You're making excuses for your bad decisions."

Rova said, "Venus, you complain a lot."

"That is the way I am. Better get used to it."

Rova clenched her fist.

Inom asked, "What should we do now?"

I said, "Let's use one of the enemy ships."

Venus asked, "Who can fly them?"

I said, "Me."

Rova turned pale.

Venus looked down her nose at me.

Eve said, "So can I."

Mark blinked.

Eve said, "My last probe just ascertained that sixty percent of the enemy ship's three-D holographic controls are similar to those on Camor's bridge."

Rova asked, "Eve, was your probe thorough?"

"A valid question."

Inom asked, "Eve, are you exaggerating?"

"To the contrary."

Inom gave her a stern look. "The battle must have distracted you."

Eve said, "It did not."

Inom said, "I'll believe it when you use those three D holographic controls."

A life-size three-D holographic replica appeared close to Eve. She said, "This is based on my last probe."

Venus sighed. "It looks realistic, but it could be inaccurate."

I said, "Let's go. An enemy destroyer might be close by, ready to shoot at us."

Venus said, "Tom, you're too paranoid."

My back muscles tightened. "Venus, are you coming with us?"

She nodded. Our group trekked.

We reached the enemy ships. I pointed at an RC, one with the name *Siggen* on its starboard side. "Let's board this."

Mark scowled. "Can you really fly it?"

My jaws muscles tightened. "It's time to find out."

Venus shook her head. "You're not sure. This is no time to experiment."

I ground my teeth together, put off by her nagging. "That is an order."

She recoiled.

Ben sighed.

Eve stared at me, a vacant expression in her eyes.

Inom's brow tensed up.

Rova said, "I'm up for taking a chance."

Everybody stepped inside the vessel. Eve and I entered the bridge. Outside the window, leaves on trees jerked, pushed by the wind. Chairs rose out of the floor. We sat. In front of us, control panels, three-D floating spheres, and screens appeared.

Eve said, "These are somewhat familiar." She stuck her fingers through a floating pyramid.

"Yes, somewhat." I touched several three-D floating spheres, shapes with algorithms on them. The engine started, then roared louder. The ship jerked upward.

Eve said, "A rough take off."

"In the future, I'll do better."

"A valid remark."

The ship lunged forward, went over the jungle, and rose.

A Qio woman with orange skin, a Captain in a tan uniform appeared on a six-feet-by-six-feet yellow screen, one that was in front of Eve and me. She barked, "I'm Captain Nogo. Siggen, your take-off was sloppy. ID yourself."

I touched a sphere, shutting off a microphone, and asked, "Eve, where is the ID?"

"This might be it. XRMMT."

On a nearby screen, one that was turquoise, an enemy Viper spacecraft, a triangular-shaped vessel with the name *Echan* on its belly, enlarged.

I repeated the identification.

A laser blast struck our port side, tearing off a satellite dish. I blurted, "Eve, your answer regarding the ID was wrong."

CHAPTER THIRTY-EIGHT

She kept staring at the turquoise screen, a blank expression on her face. "Pardon my mistake."

Wanting to change this vessel's course, I stuck my hand inside a sphere. The Siggen jerked starboard. A laser blast barely missed the top of our ship.

Eve said, "Tom, that was quick thinking."

My adrenaline pumped harder. "Thanks." I lowered my hand, a couple of inches. The Siggen lurched port. A laser shot grazed the ship's tail. I quivered. "It's time to take desperate measures."

"A valid statement."

I thrust my fingers into a floating trapezoid. Our ship plummeted two hundred feet. While sweat poured down my neck, Siggen raced between trees. "The Echan is close behind us."

Eve remarked in a monotone, "Correct."

We entered a canyon. Forty feet above our craft, tiny V-shaped creatures flew over a natural bridge. As my hearted pounded, we reached an ocean's shoreline. I shoved my fingers into a floating oval, wanting to take evasive action. The Siggen dropped, struck the water, and passed seaweed. "Is Echan following us?"

"They're eighty feet away."

I clenched my teeth.

Within thirty minutes, we came upon a pair of sixty-foot long whale-like creatures, a species with gigantic dorsal fins.

131

Wanting to avoid them, I thrust my fingers inside a trapezoid, then pulled them out. Our vessel rose several feet and barely missed the alien species. "What is that on-screen four?"

"An alien predator. It just bit a chunk out of the Echan."

I exhaled, relieved.

Before long, I stuck my fingers into the trapezoid. The Siggen rose, shot out of the water, zoomed over a shoreline, then raced across a desert. A gigantic beast jumped out from behind a boulder and smashed into our vessel.

I trembled.

"The creature tore off Siggen's starboard wing."

"Everybody, prepare for impact."

Mark yelled, "Horrible."

The ship jerked downward, shaking, and slid across the sand. Before long it raced between gigantic cacti. I said, "The ship . . ." It struck a small hill, lurched upward, crashed to the ground, and kept going.

While warning lights flashed, a robot voice announced, *Kalo, rah.*

Eve announced, "That is a Qio warning, telling us to pull up."

I clenched my teeth.

CHAPTER THIRTY-NINE

Our vessel entered an arroyo, then flipped over, ended up on its side, and halted. I said, "Is anybody hurt?"

Eve said, "Not me."

Venus said, "I'm bruised. It's not serious."

Mark said, "Just a minor cut on my wrist."

Ben said, "I sprained my arm."

Not far from him, Inom said, "My neck is sore. It's no big deal."

Adjacent to Inom, Rova announced, "There is a deep cut on my chest. A few seconds ago, I sprayed a bandage on it. Then nanites entered the wound, are repairing it."

I broke into a cold sweat. "Rova let me know if there are any problems."

"I will."

I said, "Let's search for water and food." Everybody climbed out of the wreckage.

A three-D holographic cartogram, one that was three feet high, four feet wide, appeared in front of Eve. She said, "This recently- created map confirmed that there are springs due north of here, twenty-three miles away."

Venus said, "The map is probably wrong."

Inom asked, "Why do you think it's wrong?"

Venus asked, "Why are you arguing with me?"

Rova glared at her. "He wants to know why you don't trust Eve's judgment."

Venus said, "Both of you talk too much. I should be leading this group."

Mark said, "Venus, you would be a good leader."

"I would. Isn't that obvious?"

Ben grimaced. "Tom should lead."

Venus said, "Ben, you don't know what you're talking about."

He glanced at her, his eyes glazed over.

Venus shook her fist at him. "Ben, you aren't listening to me."

He shook his head.

I said, "Let's head north."

Eve said, "If we march at two miles per hour, there is a forty percent chance of reaching the springs twenty minutes before dusk."

Mark said, "This isn't a perfect plan, but it will do."

Venus grumbled.

Ben said, "Yes it will do."

Rova shrugged.

Inom said, "It's better than standing around here."

Everybody hiked while the late afternoon sun-like star cast long shadows.

Minutes later, Mark said, "It's hot. Although my suit is cooling me off, it isn't functioning at full capacity."

Venus scowled. "We should have remained in the wreckage."

Close to her, Inom said, "Our group needs water."

Venus said, "We won't get far in this heat."

Eve said, "It will be cooler in forty-five minutes."

Venus said, "I wasn't talking to you. Mind your own business."

A narrow beam of light came out of Eve's corneas and illuminated a patch of dirt.

Inom said, "Venus, you should be more polite."

"I'm being honest."

Rova said, "Honesty should be used with courtesy."

Venus said, "Rova, you talk too much."

She glared at Venus.

Ben asked, "Eve, why did your eyes project light on the ground?"

"They're mapping this area."

I sighed. "Let's focus on locating water."

Soon, we passed ironwood trees. On their branches, orange and tan primates, about three tall hooted. *Tooay, maha.*

Eve said, "This software, a tool I call TCE, short for Translation Communication Enabler, has just determined that those monkeys are asking who we are."

I asked, "Why haven't you used TCE before?"

"It was flawed. I eliminated ninety-five percent of the useless syntax three minutes ago."

I said, "Good."

Eve said, "Oom, ahal. La lo."

A translation that deciphered Eve's statement appeared in my lenses. She was telling them about us.

Within seconds, nanites in our group's central nervous systems updated our telencephalons. From this point on, everybody, including me, could understand fifty percent of what these primates, mammals who called themselves the Orez, were saying.

The Orez with the biggest ears asked, "Why have you come to the Emip desert?"

I answered.

This, Orez said, "My name is Folo."

I offered our names.

Folo asked, "Are any of you thirsty or hungry?"

Venus blurted, "Both."

Folo said, "Also, beware of the Umet."

I quivered. "Who are they?"

He drew a picture of a scorpion in the sand. "This is one of them."

Eve asked, "When will we encounter these crustaceans?"

Folo asked, "What is a crus . . ."

Inom said, "Eve's word might be hard to pronounce."

Folo paused, both ears perked up.

Inom asked, "Folo, when will our group meet these preda-tors?"

"They usually come at night."

Venus said, "More trouble."

Mark tightened his lips.

Not far from Mark, Rova glanced in several directions, a worried expression on her face.

Folo pulled eggs out of his hip-mounted pouch. "There is water inside these bolos. Sogo, bring me more bolos. Our guests are thirsty."

In the near distance, another Orez raced up a tree, grabbed several, returned, and handed them to the rest of our group.

Within seconds Orez started a fire, placed worms on sticks, cooked them, then handed the crisp meal to our entire crew.

I blinked, repulsed, stuck one in my mouth, then chewed. The snack was salty. "Very tasty," I said, hating to lie to her.

Venus asked, "Very tasty? Are you kidding?"

Inom frowned. "Don't insult our hosts."

Venus grumbled incoherently.

Rova sighed, took a bite, and choked.

Ben's nostrils flared outward.

Eve placed the meal against her neck. The food slowly broke apart, then vanished.

Mark asked, "Eve what happened to your food?"

"My skin absorbed it."

Inom said, "That is an odd way to eat."

"It is efficient."

I said, "Eve, I've never seen you eat before."

Her silver pupils turned orange.

Inom asked, "Eve, why did your eyes change color?"

"They are examining this meal's vitamin C along with its amino acids."

Rova asked, "Eve, why haven't you eaten before?"

"Four minutes ago, my skin evolved to the point where it can integrate nutrients into my bio-logic boards, central nervous system, and nanites."

I asked, "How could it integrate them before?"

"My skin integrated airborne nutrients. However, the process was slower."

Venus shrugged.

Mark offered a brief smile.

Rova's eyes narrowed. "Fascinating."

Inom cleared his throat.

At dusk, I heard a distant scraping.

Folo pointed at distant boulders. "A group of Umet has arrived, are hiding behind those."

My adrenaline pumped faster.

Without warning, sixteen Umet crawled out from behind the rocks, saliva dripping off their jaws.

Venus yelled, "Oh my god."

Inom exclaimed, "They're hideous."

Eve said, "These arachnids are moving fast."

I said, "Fire at will."

CHAPTER FORTY

Shots from our weapons struck these predators. Two of them screeched. *Veeeet, veeeet.*

Eve said, "Our weapons are not stopping them."

My knees trembled. "Eve, have you used your obliterator?"

"Not yet."

Smart bullets struck them. *Veeet, veot.*

Ben said, "Most of them keep coming."

Inom announced, "Damn."

Rova shouted, "Horrible."

Inches from Rova, Folo said, "Prepare to die."

Everybody dodged to the right. The arachnids rushed by our group, their claws snapping air.

Inom said, "We . . ."

Venus wailed, "Watch out."

All arachnids halted, then spun around.

Inom said, "They're going to attack again."

Seeds flew out of a nearby acacia tree, racing toward these predators.

I pointed at the seeds. "Why are they headed for the Umet?"

Much to my surprise, these beasts halted.

Mark said, "My arm-mounted scent collector sent an aroma into the acacia. The tree responded by firing seeds at the Umet because it assumes these creatures are threatening it."

All the Umet hooted. *Doola, doola.*

Inom asked, "Why are they making that sound?"

Folo said, "They're scared."

Venus asked, "Scared? Are you kidding?"

Folo's diamond-shaped ear quivered. "I am not kidding."

Most of the Umon raised their front legs. *Doola, sssss.*

Venus asked, "What are they saying?"

Folo said, "They are trying to frighten us."

Rova said, "They're doing a great job."

I said, "Fire."

Bullets struck several Umon. *Eeeeko, eeeeko.*

Rova said, "Several of them jerked, but they haven't left."

Inom said, "Our weapons aren't powerful enough to scare them off or injure them."

Mark said, "Their shells are thick."

Ben raised a trembling hand. "I hate this."

A few shrieked. *Yoook, yoook.*

I asked, "What are they saying?"

Folo said, "They want to attack soon."

Eve asked, "What is stopping them?"

"A good question."

Several bellowed. *Loooor, looor.*

Inom asked, "What did they say?"

"Some of them are hurt."

As my adrenaline pumped faster, all the arachnids spun around, then crawled away.

Rova said, "What a relief."

Two arachnids squawked. *Noooot, nooot.*

Ben asked, "Now, what are they saying?"

Folo said, "They are worried that nearby Vy ants will notice the scent given off by the seeds, then come here. When the Vy arrives, they will attack the Umet. Most of the Umet are afraid of the Vy."

Mark said, "I don't see any Vy."

Folo said, "They are less than a mile away, resting or

working in their burrows."

I shook.

Venus yowled, "What a hideous mess."

Folo said, "My tribe has a limited amount of food and water, can't give you any more. Your group must leave in a couple of days. If you don't your tribe will die of thirst."

Rova inquired, "Where should we go?"

Folo said, "Go north. There is a spring. It's about nineteen miles from here. Not far from it there are Olog, trees with edible roots."

Mark asked, "Folo, why don't you and your family live there?"

"We would have to cross the Zon desert, a spot where Vy are more likely to attack."

Mark cringed.

Inom sighed.

Ben examined his shaky hand.

I said, "Let's go."

Everybody departed.

Venus scowled.

Mark groaned.

Inom clenched his teeth.

A floating screen appeared above Eve's wrist.

Venus glowered. "Eve, you never get upset."

"A valid remark."

Venus said, "I don't like it. I don't trust anybody who never feels remorse, anger, or any emotion."

Eve said, "Feeling isn't part of my design."

Venus mumbled incoherently.

Shortly, our band hiked between gigantic dunes that stretched to the horizon. Nanites flew out of everybody's shoulder pads, rose above their heads, and stopped, creating floating squares, one-sixteenth of an-inch thick devices that provided shade.

Mark pushed sweat off his neck. "It's hot. My suit's cooling system broke down eight minutes ago."

Inom said, "I'm having the same problem."

Everybody else said they had the same issue.

After stepping over rocks we passed weeds. To our left, about fifty-feet beyond scattered rocks, hundreds of four-inch-long ochre ants crawled out many holes. I pointed at the insects. "Can you see them?"

Eve said, "A valid question. Those must be the Vy."

Venus shouted, "They're huge, scary."

Not far from Venus, Mark scowled. "More are coming out of the holes."

Inom grimaced. "There are thousands of them."

Adjacent to Inom, Rova glared at the insects.

Ben recoiled.

I said, "If they come within fifteen feet of us, blast them."

Eve said, "A valid instruction."

I said, "Let's keep going. We need to find the springs."

Before long thousands of the Vy formed a single file line, one that was thirty feet away from our group and started circling us.

Chills went down my spine.

Venus said, "Those insects creep me out."

Mark blinked. "They're a horrible sight."

Inom asked, "Why don't they attack?"

Eve said, "An intriguing question."

Several Vy hummed. *Monnn, monnn.*

Rova asked, "Why are they making that noise?"

A floating screen appeared on Eve's wrist. On screen, meaningless computer code scrolled. "My LD, short for Language Decipher software, can't translate those sounds."

Rova groaned.

Venus said, "Eve, you're useless."

Eve kept staring at the screen.

A screen appeared on Mark's wrist. On screen, small text enlarged. He said, "This translation has pointed out that the Vy are watching us. Two want to strike. The rest are worried, afraid that we might kill them with weapons they can't see."

Inom said, "There are too many. We can't kill all of them."

Rova sighed. "Inom is correct."

I said, "Keep moving."

In a little while, our group slogged between biomorphic boulders, ones created by wind erosion. Above us, a droning grew louder. I looked up.

Two hundred feet above this spot, a trapezoid-shaped vessel descended.

Venus pointed at it the ship. "What is that?"

Inom said, "It's a freedom fighter I Fourteen."

I remembered that an I-14 was an Intergalactic spacecraft.

Venus paused, a dour expression on her face.

The I-14 stopped three feet above nearby dirt, hovering. On its side, somebody had etched a name. *Cova.*

Forty feet away, about thirty Vy turned, then crawled toward us.

While my body went cold, I announced, "When the Vy are fifteen feet away, blast them."

On the ship's side, a hatch slid open. Inside the craft, a Qio woman hollered, "Climb aboard."

CHAPTER FORTY-ONE

Venus asked, "Should we trust this stranger?"

I said, "Take a chance or die."

Venus scowled.

Two at a time, the rest of the group hopped inside the Cova.

I, the last to enter, winced, aimed to the right, and squeezed the trigger.

Five feet away, several Vy squealed. *Eeeot, eeeot.*

One of them raced up my leg. I fired. The insect fell off. *Eeeot.*

Eve said, "Hurry." The ship rose.

Other Vy darted toward my boots.

While laser blasts, coming from other's weapons, struck them, I jumped, then landed on the ship, both hands holding onto the bottom edge of the open hatch, my feet dangling.

On my boot, a Vy screeched. *Eeeot.*

I shuddered, then looked down.

Smart bullets, coming from somebody else's gun, struck its jaw. *Eeeot.* The insect fell off, both antennae twitching.

I glanced up.

Above me, Eve stooped, grabbed my right arm, and pulled me inside.

I exhaled, releasing tension. The hatch whirred shut. At the same time, my body jerked downward.

Eve said, "We're headed for Heja's outer atmosphere." Both of us walked. The wall vanished, revealing the passenger compartment. We entered and sat.

Presently I glanced out a tiny window. It enlarged until it was thirty feet long, ten feet high. Outside, miles below us, the Zon became smaller. Without warning, Cova lurched to port. My body jerked in the opposite direction. "Why did the ship change direction?"

Venus frowned. "Who knows?"

I looked outside as the ship passed meteorites. Chills went down my spine, a shocked reaction. "The ship barely missed them."

Mark asked, "Tom, what are you talking about?"

I pointed outside.

Mark said, "The only thing I see is stars, no meteorites."

I said, "They were there a second ago."

Venus said, "Tom, you were hallucinating, seeing things that weren't there."

I shook my head, annoyed.

Within minutes, the ship flew toward a wrecked G19, a thousand-foot long intergalactic carrier. I pointed at it. "Why are we bound for that?"

Rova said, "Going there is a foolish plan. The ship is abandoned, useless."

Cova went through a gigantic hole and touched down on a gigantic deck, a dimly lit spot. Outside the window, floating debris rose.

Ahead, Inom peeked outside, a stern expression on his face.

In front of him, a hatch opened. A Qio woman with mottled orange skin, a soldier in a tan uniform, entered. "My name is Lieutenant Pra. We must wait at this location for a while. More freedom fighter spacecraft will arrive soon."

I blinked, surprised. "Why are we here? Floating parts might smash into Cova."

Pra said, "If our ship remains outside, it's easier for Veen's orbiting satellites to detect us."

Rova asked, "How many of his satellites are orbiting Heja?"

Pra glowered. "Two. However, there might be more."

I asked, "When did the satellites arrive?"

Pra said, "Two days ago."

Inom said, "An ugly situation."

Venus said, "More trouble."

My guts tightened. My lenses sent neutrinos into Pra's mind. They returned.

She, Amy Pra, an only child, was born in Tota, a country in Loang, received a bachelor's in Reconnaissance.

A year later she earned a master's degree in Battlefield Strategy. While she was there, she used five different kinds of software, tools that could predict her enemies' goals sixty percent of the time. Several months after receiving her diploma, she joined Tota's Air Force. Six weeks later, when Veen took over, she quit her job and joined the Freedom Fighters.

Beyond my peripheral vision, something clunked.

CHAPTER FORTY-TWO

I trembled, then glanced in that direction. One section of a floating wing, space junk, had bumped against our starboard side and bounced off. I pointed at the starboard side. "Did it damage Cova?"

Pra cringed, then glanced in that direction. Inches above her wrist, a floating screen enlarged until it was six feet by six feet. "Fifteen diagnostic tests have verified that the starboard side is intact." She then turned and exited the room.

Directly a voice came out of our chair-mounted speakers. "This is Captain Dest. Two Veen interceptors will arrive in less than a minute."

I recoiled.

Venus hollered, "Damn it!"

Mark clenched his teeth.

Inom jumped up. "It's time to fight."

Eve rose to her feet.

Ben paused, an agonized expression on his face.

Rova's lips tightened. "Horrible."

I glanced out the window. In the near distance, both Veen interceptors, space vessels that were thirty feet long, shaped like arrowheads, flew through a large hole and touched down, close to Cova.

Ben exclaimed, "They're here."

On both interceptors' bellies, hatches slid open. Four enemy soldiers, six-foot-tall humanoids that were dressed in camouflaged jumpsuits, jumped out of a vessel, then raced toward ours.

As my adrenaline pumped harder, I said, "Captain Dest, open this window."

Ben asked, "What is Dest waiting for?"

The window vanished.

Laser beams came out of the enemy soldier's wrist-mounted pistols. One blast grazed my arm.

I recoiled, then squeezed the trigger.

Bullets struck an enemy soldier. This stranger collapsed.

The top half of a nearby seat disintegrated.

Beyond my peripheral vision, somebody yelled, "I'm hit."

I flinched while squeezing the trigger.

Two enemy soldiers ducked.

One of their colleagues stumbled and crashed to the floor. Without warning, all of them spun around, darted toward their interceptors, and hopped inside. While their engines boomed, all the enemy ships rose and took off.

Eve said, "My quantum computer is trying to figure out why they departed."

Ben said, "Eve, you're a great shot."

Venus said, "She was lucky."

Inom said, "Eve, your aim was excellent."

Venus said, "Others fought as hard as she did."

Rova said, "Venus, give her more credit."

Venus glared at Rova.

Mark said, "Eve is just a robot. Most of them are flawed."

Inom said, "Mark, you're ignoring the obvious. Eve never missed."

Mark gave Inom the finger.

Inom said, "I've seen that hand signal before. Insulting me won't change the fact that Eve is a talented colleague."

I said, "Cova should leave now. More interceptors might return soon."

Eve said, "There is a thirty-nine percent they will return

soon."

Mark said, "I assumed that the orbiting satellites didn't spot us because we were inside this wreck."

Ben said, "They could have noticed Cova before it entered this craft."

Mark's jaw muscles tightened. "Maybe."

The End

To be continued

YOU MAY ALSO ENJOY THE FOLLOWING FROM DEVINE DESTINIES:

Starship Fane
Thadd Evans

Excerpt

I sat, my adrenaline pumping, worried about the future. In the last several hundred years, many stars had cooled off. At the same time, the surface temperature of nearby planets had dropped below zero. As a result, trillions of humans, Aito, and members of other races had perished. Although scientists on these planets had told millions of leaders to build galactic vessels, ones that would transport residents to warmer planets, only about eight thousand leaders paid attention.

Without warning, my contact lenses beeped, indicating that somebody was calling me. Dr. Hume, the head of a team of scientists named the NAA, the National Association of Astronomers, appeared in them. He frowned. "Captain Adam Fiirs, you have a new assignment. You will be the pilot of the new Starship Fane, a craft that will leave soon. Three members of the NAA team liked your resume because you along with your crew landed the spacecraft Leenad on the Wen Et space station without any problems, the only pilot who has ever done that."

"Thank you, sir."

"At any rate, NAA astronomers have recently spotted two habitable planets, Yerak and Isal. Unfortunately both are light years away, so far from us that it's impossible to determine what specific life forms are on them.

"The Lergo, a new starship with two thousand passengers, will leave tonight bound for Yerak. Yours, the Fane, a much smaller craft, will leave not long after Lergo departs." He paused.

I nodded, sweating. According to a recent newspaper headline, gamma rays would strike our planet Laasp in the near future, slaughtering billions of people on all three of its continents, yerr, laz, and toha along with both of its largest islands, fot and ry.

"Talk to as many potential crew as possible. Tell us if you think they're qualified. Since there isn't much time and HR staff are busy, a PSR will pick the rest."

My mind sped up, trying to anticipate how many problems would pop up before Fane left. Would PSR, personnel selection robots, pick the best employees?

Hume stood, glowering. "If you have any questions, contact me. I have to attend a meeting with President Gravin in a few minutes."

I offered a forced grin while he rushed off. Text along with a 3D hologram of Eaaga, a co-pilot, an Aito woman with blue skin, appeared in my lenses. When she was a teenager, this professional discovered math on a website. In three months she used differential calculus to design two types of shaping shifting shuttlecraft. She received straight A's in high school.

She attended Moro, a university where she received a Bachelors of Science in Math, a Masters in Science in Math and a doctorate in Space Vector Analysis. Several months after graduating, Intra Corporation hired her and she along with her co-pilot began operating the Gull, an eighty-foot long spacecraft that transported spectrometers, food and medical supplies to and from barmo, zaol, and lyen, Laasp's three moons. They did this for five years.

Four months after reaching zaol, she figured out how to use nonlinear equations along with four software applications to create better routes between all three moons.

I sent her an email, telling this potential colleague about my desire to interview her in person for this job. A 3D hologram of her came out of the background. "I'm ready. Come right over."

I entered the Gull's cockpit. It took off. In front of me, Eaaga sat, her brow tight in concentration. She shoved her hand through a holographic screen.

I sat. "Have you read all of the job's requirements?"

She glared at me. "Of course. I feel that I'm more qualified for this position than anybody else."

I looked out the window while the ship zoomed over a twenty thousand-foot high mountain. As my adrenaline pumped, the craft went between two galactic personnel transporters, decelerated and docked on a planetary equipment carrier. I said, "How many types of spacecraft have you piloted?"

She blurted, "Eight. I just sent videos about this into your contact lenses."

In my lenses, the first, the Sorm, a fifty-foot long reconnaissance vessel, one that resembled a bullet, flew inside a moon's crater and landed.

I blinked, impressed. "Excellent. You're hired."

"What's next?"

"My assistant will send you an email regarding that question in a few minutes." I departed. The resume of Reoda, a potential crewmate scrolled through my lenses. This female human, a candidate with a Bachelors degree in Galactic mapmaking, a Masters in Data Analysis and Doctorate in Astrophysics was a navigator on eight galactic freighters, ships that transported medical equipment and other goods to and from barmo, zaol, and lyen.

The personnel carrier Yoon docked inside Space Station Glaan's largest hangar. I climbed out, walked, entered a cafe and sat at a table.

On the opposite side, Reoda glowered. "You're late."

I winced. "Sorry. There was a lot of traffic."

"That's a lousy excuse."

My stomach muscles tightened, an irritated response.

"According to my records, Fane hasn't been thoroughly tested in deep space. Is that correct?"

I leaned back, put off by her lousy attitude. "That is correct."

She banged her fist on the table. "As far as I'm concerned, this is a suicide mission."

I bit my lip, frustrated.

She glared at me. "Is there another ship, one that has been field tested more thoroughly, available?"

"No."

This scientist blurted, "Then forget about it. Find somebody else." She rose and stomped off.

My mind sped up, trying to figure out what I would do if the other potential candidates rejected my offer.

A 3D hologram of Duane Goam along with his resume scrolled through my lenses. This Qio humanoid, a man with purple skin, graduated from Lowan high school at the top of his class. He attended Karn, a university in the Sen Republic, a country in toha. He received a Bachelors in Mechanical Engineering, a Masters in Object Programming along with a doctorate in Fusion Engine Statistics from this school. Days after graduating, he moved to laz, and started working for Membo, a company that built and repaired galactic motors, engines designed for spacecraft.

I paused, impressed, then sent him an email, asking him if he wanted to be interviewed. His blurred face, an incoming call, focused. He scowled. "We can meet in forty minutes. However, I haven't studied the job requirements. I'll look at them in a few seconds."

I entered a hangar, near the top of Space Station Nas, and walked toward a twenty-foot long fusion engine. In the near distance, Goam climbed out of a twenty-foot high RMR, routine maintenance robot, an android used to repair and update fusion engines. Nanites rose of the floor and went together, creating a room, a quiet place where both of us could talk. We strolled through its liquid like wall and sat at a table.

I said, "Does the job interest you?"

He raised an eyebrow. "Although Fane needs more field testing, we have to leave Laasp soon. I don't look forward to the journey. But that's just the way it is. Yes, I'm interested. Will you contact me soon regarding the next step?"

"My assistant will send you an email regarding that question in a few seconds."

Goam sighed. "That is acceptable."

I departed. Dr. Mary Browna's vita along with her 3D holographic ID materialized. This human had received a Bachelors and Masters in Physiology from Leam, a college in the United Provinces, a school in Yerr. She, a primary care physician, had received her medical degree from Ossen, a university in the Maas Republic, a country in yerr. She graduated third in her class.

Noem, a hospital in Maas' capital Ima, hired her several days after graduating. She studied the after effects of primary cosmic rays on humans, Qio and Aito humanoids for eight years, wanting to find out if their immune systems could be enhanced to the point where the rays wouldn't kill them. On some occasions she used alginate to place cells in the body, a technique that cured melanoma, leukemia and other diseases.

During this time she programmed and used MEC, medical care androids, robots that helped her treat more patients. Eight years ago, she was transferred to Kab, a hospital that was understaffed.

The Yoon, a shuttle touched down on Secm, a transportation hub on zaol. A hatch opened. I left the Yoon, rushed across a platform, entered a maglev train, and sat next to other passengers. It departed. Soon it sped up, zoomed through a liquid like wall and went over zaol's barren surface, bound for a huge crater.

Within minutes, it went over the crater's rim, descended, went through a door made of nano robots and touched down, close to Kab. I stepped off the train, walked through an entrance, then sat. Nanites came out of the floor, creating a room, a table and another chair.

Dr. Browna darted inside and plopped down. She blurted, "Sorry I'm late. The operation lasted much longer than my computer model indicated."

My stomach muscles tightened, a frustrated response. "I understand."

She glowered. "Why didn't you contact me via three D holographic messaging?"

"I prefer face to face meetings."

This potential colleague paused, an irritated expression on her face.

"Did you get a chance to look over the job's guidelines?"

She sighed. "A little. However, judging by the mess we're in, it's the best option available. I don't want to die in a gamma burst. When do we leave Laasp?"

I repeated my instructions.

She exhaled, a tired expression on her face. "See you soon." I departed. Dr. Len Croll's resume and 3D holographic ID scrolled through my lenses. He, a Qio, received a Bachelors and a Masters in Astrophysics from Raem, a college in Great Ra, a country in fot. This talented student graduated with honors. He received a doctorate in Astronomy from Paoll, a university in Great Ra.

Two days after graduating, Xea Incorporated hired him. For the next three years, he operated MCIT, Multiple capability radio and optical interferometric telescopes, equipment that used the entire sound spectrum along with infrared, visible, and ultraviolet refracted light to map six planets. During this time, he along with his team of MM, mapmaking, robots used spectrometers and laser Doppler scanners to examine strange attractors along with hydrogen, oxygen, helium, and other gas ratios in all six planet's atmospheres.

I sent him an email. His 3D holographic response appeared. His jaw muscles tightened. "I'm on Iyen, charting four red giant stars. Your email regarding a job on the Fane was intriguing."

"I would like to interview you face to face, but you're a long way from here."

He clenched his teeth. "Interview me right now. I'm too busy to leave this area."

I bit my lip, irritated that we couldn't talk about this in person. "If you wish. Does the job interest you?"

He sighed. "Although I want to stay on Iyen, it's important to be practical. In other words, if I don't join your crew, I'll die."

I nodded.

"When and where do I go?"

I repeated my instructions.

He grimaced. "See you soon." The hologram vanished. I sent an email to Dr. Hae Lana, an Aito humanoid with turquoise skin, a woman who spoke five languages. Her text response scrolled. According to it she received Bachelors in three languages, English, Aito, and Qio from Wen, a college in Bema, a country in fot. She also attended Hart, a university in Noma, a country in laz. After attending Hart for three years, she earned a Masters in Physics. In her thesis, she wrote about gravitational pull inside twenty different spacecraft. She received a doctorate in Computer Science from Hart. For her dissertation she wrote Langco, software that analyzed the differences and similarities between three languages, English, Aito, and Do Ga.

Her face, another response, came out of my lenses' background. She offered me a brief smile. "I'm aboard the shuttle-craft Yean, preparing to teach a class. I glanced over your email, thought it was worth examining. Can you meet me in three hours?"

"Yes."

"Good, see you then."

ABOUT THE AUTHOR

I'm retired, used to work in market research. When I'm not writing, I paint pictures and draw. This is my website.
http://thadd.net/wr.html